The Afterwards

A.F. HARROLD
Illustrated by EMILY GRAVETT

BLOOMSBURY
CHILDREN'S BOOKS
NEW YORK   LONDON   OXFORD   NEW DELHI   SYDNEY

BLOOMSBURY CHILDREN'S BOOKS
Bloomsbury Publishing Plc
50 Bedford Square, London WC1B 3DP, UK

BLOOMSBURY, BLOOMSBURY CHILDREN'S BOOKS and the Diana logo
are trademarks of Bloomsbury Publishing Plc

First published in Great Britain in 2018 by Bloomsbury Publishing Plc

'Arrangements' by Douglas Dunn from Elegies (© Douglas Dunn, 1985)
is printed by permission of Faber and Faber Ltd
'Arrangements' by Douglas Dunn from Elegies (© Douglas Dunn, 1985)
is printed by permission of United Agents (www.unitedagents.co.uk) on behalf of Douglas Dunn

A catalogue record for this book is available from the British Library

ISBN: HB: 978-1-4088-9431-6; TPB: 978-1-4088-9968-7; eBook: 978-1-4088-9432-3

2 4 6 8 10 9 7 5 3 1

Printed and bound in China by C&C Offset Printing Co. Ltd
Shenzhen, Guangdong

To find out more about our authors and books visit www.bloomsbury.com
and sign up for our newsletters

The Afterwards

Also by A.F. HARROLD

The Imaginary
Illustrated by EMILY GRAVETT

The Song From Somewhere Else
Illustrated by LEVI PINFOLD

A tidy man, with small, hideaway handwriting,
He writes things down. He does not ask,
'Was she good?' Everyone receives this Certificate.
You do not need even to deserve it.

Douglas Dunn
from 'Arrangements'
Elegies (Faber 1985)

Hear and attend and listen; for this befell and behappened and became and was, O my Best Beloved, when the Tame animals were wild. The Dog was wild, and the Horse was wild, and the Cow was wild, and the Sheep was wild, and the Pig was wild – as wild as wild could be – and they walked in the Wet Wild Woods by their wild lones. But the wildest of all the wild animals was the Cat. He walked by himself, and all places were alike to him.

Rudyard Kipling
from 'The Cat That Walked By Himself'
Just So Stories

PROLOGUE

An old woman returns to a town she once knew.

It is a bright day. A summer's day.

From the train station she gets a taxi to an ordinary street. Stops outside a shop that was once a bakery. Gets out. Looks in the window at the absence of doughnuts.

It takes time to walk from there to the mouth of the alley. Much longer than it used to take. But then, everything takes longer now. Walking, making tea, getting out of bed.

The sound of children playing echoes in the blue sky from a field somewhere, or a playground.

She unfolds a sheet of paper from her coat pocket.

It had been forgotten for such a long time, but recently, after Mo died, and after talking to the doctor, it had risen to the top of her desk drawer. It had found its way to her hand.

She steps forward, the paper cold in the warm sunlight.

It *is time*, she thinks. It's *been long enough now*.

She walks by herself, into the alley.

She is looking forward to seeing the cat one more time.

She wants to say 'Thank you' at last.

December ran up the stairs two at a time, tripping at the top and knocking a pile of paperbacks over as she caught herself.

She spun on the landing, ignoring the books, and hurtled into her bedroom.

Her hair was wet and dripping and she plunged her head into a towel that had been warming on the radiator.

'Ah!' she said

Luxury.

She'd been looking forward to this for ages, thinking about it the whole journey home.

It had obviously been about to rain, but her dad had insisted they go for a walk in the woods anyway. It was what families did on a Sunday afternoon, and they *were* a family, after all.

'It's a beautiful day,' he'd said. 'I wouldn't be surprised if the bluebells are out. This is just the weekend for it.'

The bluebells *had* been out, whole rippling beds of them underneath the trees, but so had the clouds and they'd got absolutely soaked.

It had been a long walk back to the car without an umbrella.

She hadn't spoken to him on the way home.

'Shoes!' he shouted from downstairs.

The front door banged shut.

She sat on her bed and looked at her shoes.

She'd scraped the worst of the mud off before they got in the car, of course, but they still weren't exactly what you'd call clean. And they certainly weren't dry by any stretch of the imagination.

There were dark footprints leading across the carpet straight to her.

Well, it was *his* fault, she reckoned, not feeling very guilty at all. If he'd had a warm, clean towel in the car, she wouldn't have needed to hurry upstairs to dry her hair. So she wasn't to blame. Not really.

She bent down and tugged at the laces. They didn't budge.

'Knots!' she shouted.

'Ember,' her dad said from the doorway. 'There's no need to shout. I'm right here.'

He was holding the books in his hand. He set them down on the corner of the chest of drawers.

He smiled at her.

'Look at this carpet,' he said, shaking his head. 'You don't half take after your mum. Just like her.'

He knelt down and lifted one of her feet.

'Knots, you say?'

December nodded.

His fingers prised at the laces for a few seconds, and then he said,

'There you go.'

She wriggled out of the shoe and lifted the other one for him to untie too.

'What do you say?' he asked.

'What's for tea, Harry?' she replied, deadpan.

He stood up and poked her on the nose.

'Bangers and mash,' he said.

She watched as he picked his books up, the wet shoes dangling by their laces from the same hand, and went out on to the landing, pulling her door to behind him.

The 'What's for tea?' business was an old routine and they both liked it. It was easier than saying 'Thank you' and meant more or less the same thing. You just had to remember not to do it when you were stood in front of the headmaster's desk.

His name was Harry (and that was what she'd always called him, ever since she was little) and it was hard to stay mad at him for long. It was something about his smile, the width of it, the easiness of it, the quickness of it, the warmth of it. It was like a big, wobbly hot-water bottle looking at you.

December had known him ever since she was a baby – he was her dad, after all – and for as long as she could remember it had just been him and her. Her mum had gone away and they'd been left on their own, her and Harry, Harry and her.

And it was all right.

That's what she thought. She knew it was all right because of that smile of his.

Her best friend from school, Happiness, had a dad *and* a mum, and they were always shouting at one another, even when December went and stayed over. She'd snuggle in her sleeping bag on Happiness's floor and listen to the noise downstairs. It was a strange way to go to sleep.

Harry never shouted at her mum. Her mum never shouted at Harry. Harry never had a bad word to say about her mum. He didn't say *much* about her, but when he did he smiled and looked at December and shook his head in a way that smelt of love.

She knew she was lucky. She felt lucky.

Having a dead mum meant even the teachers at school tried to be extra nice to her, even that time when she'd tripped up Emerald Jones in the playground accidentally-on-purpose and her tooth had come out. She got what they called 'the benefit of the doubt'.

All in all, life being December wasn't so bad.

'Deck! Deck!'

Happiness was shouting in the front garden.

December opened the door, feeling slightly embarrassed as usual.

Why Happiness couldn't ring the doorbell like a normal person she wasn't sure, but it had ever been thus.

They'd lived next door to one another for nearly three years and for most of that time they'd been best friends. Ness had thrown a football at a dog that had been chasing December a few weeks after she and Harry had moved in, and that was how they'd met.

Now they were in the same class at school and sat at the same table. Their hands usually went up to answer questions at the same time. Sometimes they shared answers to tests if Miss Short was looking the other way.

They swapped their packed lunches round because sometimes you needed a break from the same sandwiches and they always snapped their chocolate biscuits in two.

This Monday was the first day back after the Easter holidays and Ness had been away visiting her grandparents for the last week, so there was lots to talk about. She was excited and bouncing on her toes as they walked down the three streets that led to school.

It was all 'Then Grandpa let out this most enormous –' and 'The dog fainted, and then Gran –' and 'Mum was so embarrassed when he said –' and the like.

December dragged her heels and laughed at her friend. She could've listened to this sort of thing forever, but soon they passed through the school gates and the bell went and the register was taken and gossip had to be put to one side for a time.

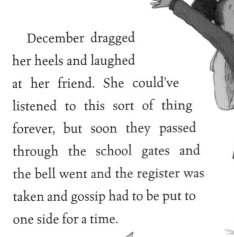

In class they learnt about the Vikings. Then they climbed ropes in the gym.

They played football at lunch and December swapped her ham sandwich for Happiness's ham roll.

In the afternoon a light rain speckled the classroom windows, but it stopped by home time. There were hardly even any puddles to splash in on the way home. And so they walked together, dry-footed, skipping and swapping stories.

Yet again it hadn't been a bad day at all.

They parted on the pavement outside their houses.

'You wanna come to the park?' Happiness asked.

'Can't,' said December. 'Going out with Dad and Penny later. Gonna have to wrap a box of chocolates first, *and* have a wash.'

'Well, see ya tomorrow then.'

'Yeah, see ya.'

Penny was Harry's girlfriend. (Although 'girlfriend' was hardly the right word, since she was over thirty, but no one seemed to notice that.)

She was nice. Didn't try to be December's mum. Didn't try to be her bestest best friend. She was just cool. Friendly enough, nice enough, kind enough.

Tonight they were going out for a meal since it was the one-year anniversary of December walking in on them kissing in the kitchen and finding out her dad had a girlfriend. If that wasn't worth going out for a meal with starters *and* afters she didn't know what was.

That night December had a strange dream.

It was last summer and she and Harry and Happiness had gone out for the day.

This had actually happened. The dream was just a repeat, as far as she could tell.

They were driving through the safari park when all of a sudden there was a bang and the car had slumped and there was this weird scraping noise and Harry had said a word that had made December say, 'Harry, I'm shocked,' in a way that had made him laugh.

They had a flat tyre.

'Must've driven over something sharp,' he said. 'A stone or something.'

'Shall we get out and have a look?' December said, her hand already on the door handle.

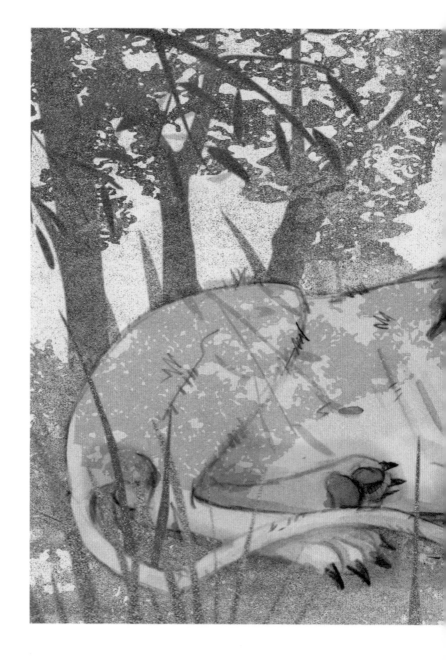

'No, Deck,' said Happiness quickly. 'I don't think that'd be a great idea.'

She was pointing out the window at the lions who were lazing in the shade beneath the tree.

'Spoilsport,' said December.

'Actually,' said Harry, 'I think Happiness makes a very good point and you should listen to her wise words.'

Ness stuck her tongue out at her friend and said, 'See? Wise words!'

'So what we gonna do?'

Harry fiddled with the gear stick and tried driving forward but the noise was horrible.

'I'll ruin the wheel if I keep on,' he said.

The car behind them honked its horn. Twice. Then it pulled out and drove round them.

Harry put the hazard lights on and said, 'We just have to wait.'

'Let sleeping lions lie,' Happiness said, keeping an eye on the lions lying in the shade.

One of them was looking up, a rather scruffy-looking one with a shaggy old tatty mane, but the sunshine was bright and hot and the big cat didn't look like it was about to move.

Ember didn't like the way the cat looked at her though, as if it knew more than she did.

After ten minutes a truck from the safari park came and towed them out of the lions' enclosure and soon the car was in the car park and they were in the café and Harry was talking to the emergency repair people on the phone.

The girls played hide-and-seek among the plastic animals, tables, vending machines and visitors that filled the noisy hall, while stuffing hot dogs in their faces.

December hid behind a fat lady and moved when she moved and got almost all the way to the door before Happiness pointed at her and shouted, 'Found you!'

'You should've seen her face,' Ness laughed when they were back in the car later on. 'She thought I was pointing at her, but I wasn't, and she got all huffy and stuck her nose in the air and her chins wobbled and she waddled off, leaving you just stood there.'

'It was a good hiding place though,' December said. 'You've got to admit, yeah?'

'Better than behind a skinny bloke,' Ness laughed.

December laughed too and then she tried to explain to Harry as he opened the door and climbed into the driving seat, but the words didn't come out right and he didn't get it, but he smiled in the mirror and said, 'Very good, girls. Seat belts on. Chop, chop.'

And they drove home.

'I spy with my little eye, something beginning with "Q",' Ness said.

'Um. Koala?'

'No.'

'What about quince?'

'What's quince?'

'It's a sort of fruit, I think,' said December.

'Nope,' said Ness.

There was silence for a while and the girls both looked out of the windows at the motorway whizzing past. Green verges and green fields, sheep and trees, and the stretching blue, cloudless and endless above. The windows were open and the air was cool and fierce on their faces, and as they passed other cars they stared at the people who refused to look back at them, and they laughed.

'Qualllm?' December said eventually.

'What's qualllm?' asked Ness.

Yes, what is qualllm? thought December,
       and then she realised she was
           yawning and the car seat
               was so soft and warm and,
                   almost mumbling,
                       she listened to herself say,

'It's that bit when you're just falling asleep

                                or just waking up

and you're all peaceful and dozy and you're lying there

and you don't really remember what's real

                                and what's not,

but it's all quite lovely.'

  'Yes,' said Ness, yawning wide, 'maybe that's it.

Falling asleep.

                 Waking up.

Maybe that's it.

          Maybe that's what it is.'

The next morning all was silent outside the house.

Silent apart from the occasional car passing by and Mr Dibnah's dog, who had a daily walk before breakfast – a walk which neither Mr Dibnah nor the dog enjoyed.

When it was time to go to school, December went and knocked on Ness's door.

There was no reply.

This was odd.

'Maybe she's already gone,' Harry said.

'But without me?'

He just grinned and shrugged his shoulders.

'You'll be all right walking on your own, yeah?'

'Of course,' she said, pulling her bag up on to her shoulder and setting off.

'Remember to wash behind your ears,' her dad called, which

was his way of saying 'Love you' and 'Goodbye for now' all in one.

December walked quickly.

When she got to school, Ness wasn't there either.

Not in the playground, not in the classroom.

They all marched through into the hall for a special assembly.

They didn't normally have assembly on a Tuesday.

'What's going on?' December asked Toby, who was in front of her as they walked down the corridor.

'Dunno,' he said, picking his nose. 'Prob'ly a vis'ter or somefink. Maybe we're gettin' prizes or somefink.'

December looked around as they walked and wondered what sort of prizes the prizes might be.

When they were all sat down in the hall, legs crossed neatly and eyes facing forward, Mr Dedman, the head, wheeled himself out in front of the crowd.

He coughed.

He looked at them.

He looked at a sheet of paper in his lap.

He coughed again.

It was as if he didn't quite know what he was doing, which wasn't like him at all. He must've taken hundreds of assemblies in his time. You could tell because his moustache had turned grey.

Despite his name he was usually friendly and made bad jokes.

Today he made no jokes.

'Um, children,' he said, without saying 'Good morning' first. (A few little voices near the front tried echoing back the usual 'G o o d m o r n i n g , e v e r y b o d y' but they stumbled to silence halfway through.) 'Children, as some of you may have already heard, um, I've got some bad news to tell you. Last night … yesterday, after school, one of our friends, one of the brightest and liveliest girls in this school, had a … an accident. She fell off a swing in the park and hit her head. It was nobody's fault, just an accident and a very sad one. The ambulance came and took her to hospital, of course, but I'm sorry, um, to say she didn't wake up again, and in the early hours of this morning she … er, she passed away.'

There was a tremor in his voice as he spoke. A tear on one cheek. His serious grown-up face went a little wobbly as December watched. His moustache trembled and sparkled. She tried to listen to his words, but they didn't quite make sense. Who was he talking about? He hadn't said anyone's name.

She was sat next to Toby, who was still picking his nose. She didn't normally sit next to Toby.

A stone was sinking inside her.

Somewhere near the front of the hall she could hear crying.

It wasn't Mr Dedman, but some of the little kids.

'We've sent a text out to your parents,' the head went on. 'I know some of you might want to be with your families today instead of here. But I want you to know that we are your family too. The whole school is here for you, and if anyone wants to talk, please remember we are here to listen. You can talk to any of us.'

'Please, Mr Dedman,' someone said. It was a child's voice.

December looked around to see who had spoken, whose hand was in the air, and discovered it was her.

'Yes, Ember?'

'You've … you've not said her name, Mr Dedman. You've not said who it is.'

'Oh.' He looked down at his hands, coughed, looked at the wall and then at December. 'I'm sorry,' he said. 'Happiness Browne. It

was Happiness who had the accident.'

There were more tears and gasps around her. A chattering sprang up, quiet, subdued, strangled, nervous, scared, and it wasn't hushed by the teachers sitting at the edge of the hall.

The stone that had been

    sinking

      inside her

        hit

          bottom.

            Mud puffed up.

             She couldn't move.

             It was

              too

                heavy.

                  'Oh,'
                  she said.

She had a quiet lunch with her dad.

He'd come and picked her up from school when he'd got the message.

'Do you want to stay?' he'd asked.

She'd shook her head. School echoed with Happiness. It was too sad.

That afternoon, Penny came round to see them.

She brought cake.

She didn't know what to say.

They sat and watched television for a bit, December curled up against her dad.

The man on the screen was learning to tap dance, but wasn't very good at it.

The cake sat on the coffee table uneaten.

After a bit, Harry said, 'Not a good day, is it? I bumped into your Uncle Graham at the shops this morning. Betty got hit by a car last night.'

'Oh no,' said Penny, 'that's awful.'

Graham was December's mum's brother. He lived nearby but they didn't see each other all that often. Betty was his dog.

She was one of those dogs that's mostly shoulders and dribble. December had never much liked her.

'I'm sorry,' she said anyway.

'Oh, pet, it's not your fault,' said Penny, getting up. 'Shall I make us some more tea?'

And so the grey day went on.

It rained in the early evening, but had stopped by the time she went upstairs.

Her dad sat on the floor by her bed and read her the report he'd been writing for work until she fell asleep. She liked it when he did that.

Soon she was snoring.

December's dreams were jumbled and distant. She had the feeling her mother had been in them, which was unusual.

She woke in the middle of the night, in the pitch dark, and heard the rain thrumming on the windows. There was a storm raging out there. She felt worried for the fishermen out at sea. She liked fish. And then, in among the thudding sting of the raindrops, she heard Happiness knocking on the glass.

Tap. Tap. Tap.

She lay there, filled with worry.

And then, later, she woke up again and it was morning. The light was shining through her curtains, which were never thick enough, never heavy enough, to the keep the day at bay.

When she opened them and looked out, the pavements were dry, not a puddle in sight.

December was quiet at breakfast.

Her dad didn't ask her what was wrong. He didn't need to.

Penny was there. She'd stayed the night, which she did every now and then.

Toast crunched slowly round the table.

Her dad walked her to school, leaving Penny to guard the house.

'You gonna be OK, kid?' he asked.

'Can't I stay home?' she said. 'I don't feel very well. I'm scared. Like butterflies.'

'I know,' he said. 'But you've gotta go. You need to go to school, and you'll be with your friends. They probably feel like you do. Don't you think?'

She kicked a dandelion that was growing out of the pavement, snapping its head off with a satisfying *snick*.

'Dunno,' she said. 'I think I just want to go back to bed. I didn't sleep well.'

'Darling,' her dad said, 'Happiness wouldn't want that, would she? She'd want you to go to school. She'd want you to be with your friends, to be with *her* friends.'

'But, Harry,' December said, 'it doesn't matter what she wants. She's not here, is she? And anyway, she liked sleeping. It was one of her most favourite hobbies.'

'Of course it matters,' her dad said, squeezing her hand. 'Of course it matters what she wants, or what she wanted. And, well ... sometimes you have to guess. You have to guess, now that they're not here to tell you. You have to work it out yourself, and you do your best to do right by them.' He paused to cough a little cough. 'Ember, my love, you just try your best to do what they would have wanted.'

'You're squeezing my hand,' she said. 'You're hurting.'

He let go.

'Sorry,' he said.

She didn't ask him what all *that* was about. She thought she understood, thought she understood why it sounded as if he cared so much. He wasn't talking about Happiness any more; he was talking about her mum.

'I'm sorry too,' she said quietly.

He never talked like that normally. He usually smiled and laughed when he talked about her mum, telling December how much fun she was, how smart, how funny. He always stopped talking before it got sad, or before he got sad, although that didn't stop December from sort of missing this woman she hardly remembered, this woman she'd hardly met.

Sometimes she looked at the photo of the three of them which sat on the mantelpiece and filled that familiar grinning stranger with all the stories her dad had told her, and, yes, it was a shame she wasn't there to tuck her in at night or to wash her hair or to mend the slow puncture her bike kept getting, but it wasn't the end of the world. Her mum wasn't there in the same way a character off the telly isn't there: you might feel you know them, you might know loads about them, you might think you probably love them even, but you don't expect them to turn up to tea one day, and if they did you probably wouldn't know what to say to them anyway.

Happiness was different though. She *should* be there. Every day. And now she wasn't.

School was odd.

The day went by as days do, but quietly. Everyone was quiet. The teachers, the kids, the dinner ladies. It was a bit like being on an old ship lost at sea, becalmed and bobbing.

Eventually the final bell went and it was home time.

Her dad wasn't waiting for her at the gates, but that was quite normal. She and Ness walked home together usually. It was only a couple of streets, after all.

Today, however, she'd secretly hoped Harry would be there. She didn't fancy walking by herself.

She knew that if she'd asked him, he'd've been there, but she hadn't asked.

She pulled her bag higher up on her shoulder, and, taking a deep breath, walked out of the playground and into the road, heading for home.

'Yo, Amber,' a voice said, just as she turned the first corner. 'Where're you off to?'

Walking towards her was a man, short and stubbly, with a blonde ponytail. He was wearing a leather jacket and dark glasses and smelt faintly of dust and cigarettes.

It was her mum's brother, Uncle Graham. In ten years, he'd never once got her name right.

He rode a motorbike that took blood samples or donor hearts or other special things between hospitals, but he didn't have his bike with him this afternoon.

'Soz I'm late, mate,' he said. 'I wasn't sure what time you got out. Back in my day we were at school right up till it got dark.' He laughed, a little yapping sort of laugh that was always a surprise when she heard it come out of him.

'Your dad sent me. Him and Whatsername've gone off for the afternoon.'

December didn't say anything. She just listened, holding the strap of her bag tightly between her fingers and thumb. The fabric was a nice sort of rough.

'He said they'll be back about six. You can come have tea at my place. Keep me out of trouble, eh?' He laughed again.

It wasn't like her dad to go off without telling her, but she couldn't very well argue with Graham. He was her uncle and she'd been round his house before, although not very often. He only lived a few roads away from her school, but in the opposite direction to home.

Besides, she didn't have a door key, so it was either go round Uncle Graham's or sit on her front step until her dad came home.

She looked up at the clouds.

They were grey, and some of them looked grumpy.

'OK,' she said. 'But it's Ember, not Amber.'

'Course it is,' laughed her uncle, slapping her on the back. 'Course it is.'

As they walked he kept up a stream of chatter, which filled the air around them.

It reminded her of walking with Ness, except he talked less about crisps and more about TV shows she'd never seen.

December watched telly in Uncle Graham's front room while he pottered around the house doing other things. He'd made her squash and a surprisingly good tuna sandwich.

She sat on the settee with her feet tucked up underneath her. She leant her head on a cushion.

It was hard to concentrate on the programme, because her mind was elsewhere. It was as if there was something she'd forgotten to do, that she'd promised someone she'd do … something important. But she checked through and counted off on her fingers and there wasn't anything. Not really. It was just … just Happiness, she guessed.

She hadn't cried yet.

That had surprised her.

She'd've wanted people to cry for her if she died.

So maybe, she thought, that meant that Happiness *wasn't* dead.

That Mr Dedman had got it wrong in assembly and had meant to say another girl's name instead and Ness had just gone off on holiday without telling anyone.

She looked at the dog basket that was on the floor by the gas fire. The blanket was dirty and dangled half out. A rubber bone lay in the very centre of the basket, not saying anything.

'You 'K, Amber?' Graham said, poking his head round the door.

He had a mug in his hand that he was drying with a tea towel.

He gave her a smile that she recognised, not because it was his smile, but from the photo of her mum at home. They had the same smile.

'D'ya want more squash or 'nother biscuit or something?' he said. 'Give it half an hour and I'll walk you home.'

'Biscuit, please,' she said.

He went away and came back with a packet of custard creams. 'Take a couple,' he said.

Half an hour later she put her shoes on.

A phone rang.

It wasn't hers because she didn't have one, even though she'd asked her dad for one a hundred times. 'Maybe next birthday,' he'd said each time.

Graham ran past, springing up the stairs, his mobile buzzing in his hand.

'Yeah?' he said as he reached the landing. 'Oh really? … Oh no … Of course, of course … I'll let you know if I see …'

He was moving about upstairs as he talked, his voice fading in and out of earshot.

Ember went into the kitchen to pick up her school bag and when she came back into the hall, Graham was just coming down.

A dog lead made of shiny silver chain hung from a hook by the front door.

The house smelt of Betty, even though she wasn't there.

She guessed the house next door to hers would smell of Happiness, even though she didn't smell.

'Out the back,' Graham said. 'We'll go out the back. It's quicker that way.'

They went through into the kitchen and out the back door.

He locked it behind them.

The garden was just a long square of earth, with sprigs of grass and weeds poking up here and there, and with a washing line crossing it diagonally.

'I keep meaning to do something with it,' he said. 'Our mum always had it beautiful, but Betty won't be doing with flowers. She's a digger. Always digging for gold.'

He gave a chuckle and shook his head.

At the end of the garden was a gate that led them out into an alley.

Graham pulled a bit of paper from his pocket. It was scrunched up and he unfolded it sort of flat and moved it around like it was a map he was trying to find north on.

'This way,' he said, pushing past a wheelie bin.

It was odd, Ember thought, that he needed a map to get out of the alley, but she didn't say anything, not knowing what to say.

He was her mum's brother, and he *had* just made her a very decent tuna sandwich, so he deserved the 'benefit of the doubt'.

They reached a place where the alley met another one, crossing it like a T-junction.

'This way,' Graham said, turning left.

She followed.

After another twenty metres they met another alley, another T-junction.

He turned left again.

Again she followed.

Overhead, clouds drifted slowly by and she could hear a pair of pigeons cooing to one another.

Another T-junction.

Left again.

Now Ember was sure there was something odd going on. If they'd turned left and then left and then left again they should be almost back where they began. That was geometry.

'Are you sure this is the right way?' she asked.

Graham, who was a few metres ahead of her, turned and looked at her and said, 'Oh yes. This is it. It's a short cut. We're almost there. Not far now.'

Something about what he said and how he'd said it, a series of answers that tripped over each other as he'd spoken, made the hair on the back of her neck stand up.

He sounded odd. Nervous.

They went round another corner.

Should I run? she thought, and as she thought it she noticed something in the shadows.

Sat on top of a dustbin (not a wheelie bin, but one of those old-fashioned, round metal ones you see in old telly programmes) was a cat. She could hardly make it out in the gloom. It was a rough dark shape in the shadows, but she saw the flicker of its odd-coloured eyes as it slowly blinked at her. One was red; one was blue.

'C'mon,' Graham said, turning left yet again
and heading up another alley.

Not really seeing what other option
she had, Ember followed and as
she turned the corner she
looked again at the cat and
it shook its head, tattered
ears and all, as if to say,
'Don't go *that* way.'

But then it jumped
down from the bin
and padded off
in the
opposite
direction.

Graham was ahead of her,
just ten metres away
and he was opening a gate
on one side of the alley.
A gate into one of the gardens.

He looked at his piece of paper before he did so and sighed deeply.

It was an odd thing to see, that sigh, though Ember couldn't really say why.

She walked up to him.

'Are we back at *your* house?' she asked.

Turning four corners would've brought them round in a circle (well, a square), back to where they started. But she wasn't sure how many corners they'd gone round. The memory seemed muddy.

Uncle Graham didn't say anything but walked through the gate into the garden.

Looking through the gate she noticed something wrong. Something strange and wrong.

Ember had seen enough old films on the telly to know what the world looked like in black and white.

And she'd seen enough of the world to know that it was only black and white in old films.

Graham's garden (and it *was* his garden, it had the same saggy washing line across it, though the lawn looked more grassy and flowerbeds filled with flowers lined the sides) was now in black and white.

She looked at the alley around her, at the tarmac at her feet, at the wheelie bin over the way. Colour. It was all colour. Normal. Only the garden and the house beyond it were black and white. Through that gate. Not normal.

Grey and grey and grey.

'What's happened?' she said.

'Quickly,' said Graham urgently. 'Come in here, I've got

something to show you. It's important.'

She stepped through the gate.

She held her hands up in front of her face. They were still the same colour as they'd always been. So was Graham. It was just the world. (Even the sky above her was grey now, where it had been blue moments before.)

Graham unlocked the back door.

There was a noise inside. A snorting, chomping, ugly noise.

Ember took a step back, but it was just Betty, just Graham's dog, Betty, bursting out of the door in an explosion of slobber and shoulders and joy.

Graham fell to his knees and hugged her.

'Yes,' he said. 'Oh, love.'

Her tail was a crazy blur, her eyes glittered with canine adoration, her clawed feet clattered on the concrete of the back step.

She was, however, like a dog from an old film. That is to say, she was black and white, like the garden, like the house, like the world. And although she *was* a black and white dog (white with black splotches), this was something different.

They looked so happy together, Graham and Betty, as if they belonged together like a heart inside a chest. And although she'd always found the dog scary, dribbly and growly, although Betty had always looked at her from the side of her mouth like a gangster worried that someone was after her food, Ember found that the sight of the two of them together, reunited, made her smile. Warmed her.

It warmed her until she remembered.

The dog is dead.

And then she felt cold.

The dog was knocked down.

And then she felt sick.

Dead dogs wag no tails.

And then a voice spoke.

'This? You *really* want to do *this*?'

It sounded incredulous.

December spun round.

Behind her, blocking the way to the alley, was a woman.

She was tall, wide, muscly, wearing a light summer dress covered with pictures of bright flowers and skulls.

She was pointing at Ember with one hand, palm up, index finger loosely lolling in her direction.

'You would swap *this*, for *that*?'

She pointed at the dog.

Graham nodded, his hand on Betty's head, filled with love.

He didn't look at Ember.

It was almost as if he couldn't, or wouldn't.

'What's happening?' she asked, first looking at him and then at the woman. Eager to receive an answer from either one.

'Very well,' said the woman, not talking to Ember.

She stepped to one side and gestured to the back gate.

'Go. Don't look back.'

Her voice was filled with closing doors.

Graham shooed Betty out into the alley and then followed her, not looking round.

Ember thought she heard him mumble 'Sorry' as he went past, but she couldn't be sure.

Before she could move, the tall woman in the summer dress slipped through the gate into the alley too, and closed it behind her.

Ember was left in the garden. In the black and white, really weird, garden.

'Oh no you don't,' she said, getting control of herself again.

She grabbed hold of the gate handle and twisted it so the latch lifted, and pulled it open.

The alley was there, as before, except the colour wasn't and neither were the people or the dog who had, just seconds before, stepped through it.

'Oh,' she said.

December looked both ways up and down the alley.

It was grey and silent.

She stepped out and let the gate swing shut behind her.

There was no wind and her hair didn't ruffle in it.

She wondered which way she should go.

To the left, where she'd come from, was a dead end that hadn't been there before.

To the right was, instead of the corner they'd passed two minutes before, an alley-mouth that led out to a grey pavement, out to a grey street. The T-junction had disappeared.

Seeing no other choice, she heaved her school bag on to her shoulder and walked to the street.

Although it was grey and although it was silent she recognised the road. It curved round towards her school. A little way down on the other side was a newsagent's, and further along past that was a little bakery where she and Harry sometimes bought iced buns or doughnuts.

The buildings were all there and the lamp posts, but there wasn't a car to be seen, nor a person.

It was usually quite a busy road, with cars and buses going about their business, and people walking dogs or hurrying along with umbrellas or talking to a postman.

But now there was nothing. No one.

It was like Ember had woken up in a dream and everyone else had stayed asleep, as if the world had stopped and only she'd been missed out and was still moving about. She didn't like it.

It didn't make sense.

Her heart tiptoed in her chest, trying not to worry her.

Maybe if she just went home, Harry would be able to explain everything. He usually did.

So she turned in the direction of her school and started walking. Three streets past the school was home. It wouldn't take ten minutes to get there.

The two girls had been sleeping at December's house one night when they'd gone downstairs, while Harry was snoring, and drunk all the custard in the fridge. There'd been two of those big plastic tubs, which he'd bought because they'd been about to go past their sell-by date and so had been cheap.

They'd raced each other, glugging them down, and it had been a tie.

They'd crept back to bed, stifling giggles, sticky-faced and feeling swollen.

December had fallen asleep.

And she'd slept until Ness woke her up by being sick all over her sleeping bag, and then Harry had got up and dealt with everything, even though it was the middle of the night.

He might've grumbled a bit, but he hadn't been angry. He'd got the spare sleeping bag out of the airing cupboard and everyone had gone back to bed.

But when Ness's mum heard about it in the morning, she wasn't so happy. She'd shouted and pointed her finger.

'Out-of-date custard!' she'd said, shaking her head. 'Out of date! What sort of a father … ?'

Whose idea had it been to have the custard race?

December couldn't remember.

Had *she* been a bad influence on Ness or had it been the other way round?

She knew what Ness's mum would say, but she reckoned they both took the lead at different times. That was why they were such good friends. They took turns bossing each other around. Being the smart one.

But why had she thought of custard just then?

Oh!

It had been seeing the empty windows in the bakery as she went past. Normally there were trays of cakes and pastries and doughnuts, but in this grey world there'd been nothing in there. Nothing for sale. And Ness was weird. She preferred *custard* doughnuts to *jam* doughnuts.

How silly.

But maybe it was better to listen to the fluttering of a silly memory like that than the others that were lurking in the shadows and round the corners. She tried not to look at them.

And then, suddenly, as she walked she heard a noise, a clicking sound, almost a *tick-tick-tick*, and something in the corner of her eye made her turn.

There was a low brick wall keeping a front garden from spilling on to the pavement. The clicking sound came from there.

It was only a small sound, not a scary one, and December was intrigued. It was the first noise she'd heard since the world had turned black and white, since she'd been abandoned in this place.

There was a smudge in the air, a blur, on top of the wall. Not a shadow, but a brownish-charcoal smear, a hint of colour in the grey world, and it was moving. It was *something like* the shape of a bird. With every click it tapped at the concrete.

And then the bird-smudge vanished, blinked away, and something small and grey and wriggling fell to the ground.

She knelt down and saw, in the now familiar black and white, a little snail.

The tiny eyeballs rose up on the tiny eyestalks and peered around, examining her and the world, and then, after a few moments of wriggling, a wind (a wind that she didn't feel) caught hold and the snail became dust and smoke and fell apart and blew away into the air.

Gone.

'Oh,' she said,

standing up. 'Poor snail.'

She'd paid enough attention to her dad when they'd been out on Sunday walks to know that the bird-shaped smudge in the air must have been a thrush doing what thrushes do, which is cracking open snail shells to get at the snail inside. But why the bird had been a smudge and why it had simply vanished, and why the snail had been in focus and had turned to dust and blown away, she didn't know. *That* wasn't a normal part of the thrush's behaviour. Or the snail's. So far as she remembered.

She shifted the strap of her school bag on her shoulder and straightened herself up.

'OK, Ember,' she said out loud. 'Time to get moving.'

She continued on up the street, towards school and towards home, though what she'd find there in this strange empty world, this strange empty version of her world, she didn't know and wouldn't guess.

'No one's home,' said Happiness.

She'd been sitting on her doorstep, when Ember had arrived.

She looked just like the rest of the world, a girl in a black and white movie.

'I've been knocking, Deck,' she said, 'but no one answers and I don't have a key and the doors are locked and I don't understand.'

Ness was looking at Ember, but covering her eyes with her hand, as if the sun were shining in them.

Then she looked away, off to one side.

December had stopped by the wooden gate.

She didn't go into Ness's front garden but stood thinking on the pavement.

She knew she should be scared, should be afraid, but instead a big, open, confused emptiness was inside her, and her thoughts echoed.

'Ness?' she said, after a silence. 'You're supposed to be dead.'

'Oh,' said Happiness, scratching the back of her head.

Ember wondered if she shouldn't have said what she just said. What if Ness hadn't known? What if it wasn't true? What if … ?

'I thought it must be something like that,' her friend said, looking at the ground and scuffing her toe against the crazy paving of the path. 'That's why it's so quiet. What happened?'

'You fell off a swing.'

'Oh,' she said again. The way she said it made it sound like these surprises were only small ones, like finding 2p on the floor. Nothing to get excited about. 'That's a bit silly, isn't it? I've fallen off swings loads of times before without dying.'

'This time you hit your head,' Ember explained. 'Probably on one of the metal posts, I expect. Mr Dedman didn't say exactly.'

'Did it hurt?'

'I dunno. You're asking the wrong person. I should be asking *you* that.'

Happiness almost smiled, but it was a grey and hopeless attempt. She didn't look at Ember.

'I don't think it hurt. I don't remember it hurting. But then again I don't remember falling, so …'

She let the words trail off into dust.

December pushed the gate open and took a couple of steps up the path.

'I'm so sorry,' she said.

'What for?'

'For not going to the park with you. For not stopping you from dying. You know … that sort of thing.'

'Oh, I'm sure it wasn't your fault,' Happiness said. 'Accidents happen.'

'Yes, but …'

The emptiness in Ember's inside had become, as they'd talked, a whirlpool that she felt herself being drawn into.

Happiness was dead. And Betty, the dog, had been dead too. And she'd seen that snail die when the thrush had cracked open its home. And she was in this silent world. Where the dead … lived.

So the question spun itself around to face her: did that mean *she was dead too?*

She looked at her hands.

They were still the colour of a living person's hands.

Her school trousers were grey, but the usual, normal, *real* grey they'd always been, not the grey of a silent movie. Not the grey of Ness. And her jumper (oh!) was still red, bright like blood.

December wasn't dead.

She didn't feel dead.

Nothing had *happened* to make her die.

'What do we do now?' Ness said, sitting back down on the doorstep.

'I don't know,' said Ember, and she went and sat next to her friend.

She put a hand on Ness's knee.

It wasn't cold, but it wasn't warm either.

At least it was there; at least Ness wasn't just a ghost that Ember's hand passed through.

Ness pulled her knee away. Brushed at it.

'It stings,' she said. 'Sorry.'

For the first time in their friendship December wasn't sure what to say.

They sat in silence for a bit, looking out at the street, out at the houses opposite.

Over their roofs a black circle was sinking.

It was the sun.

Shadows stretched towards them across the road.

'Hang on,' said Ember. She'd just remembered something important.

She pulled her bag up and got her lunchbox out.

Something rattled inside it.

She held the chocolate biscuit up and snapped it in two.

'Halves?' she asked.

She hadn't eaten it at lunchtime because she'd not felt hungry then.

'Thanks, Deck,' said Ness, 'but I'm not hungry.'

December *was* hungry, so she ate the whole biscuit. Both halves.

And then, as she licked the last crumbs from her fingers, something happened in front of them.

On the top of the wall that separated the front garden from the street another smudge appeared in the air. A smudge like she'd seen when that thrush had killed the snail, but bigger.

It wasn't bird-shaped this time, but cat-shaped.

In the blurred jaws the distinct shape of a struggling small bird appeared.

It was a robin, Ember could tell, and it slumped, suddenly still, in the mouth of the cat – a scruffy, battered old alley cat, the sort you wouldn't want coming through your cat flap while you were having your breakfast.

It dropped the bird, shook itself, and sat up, looking at the two girls, looking solid and as real as anything.

At its feet the black and white robin fluttered, hobbled up, fit and unbroken, hopped away, leapt into the air, and flew up to perch on a telegraph wire, from where, after a few seconds, it vanished, blown away in a streaming cloud of dust, just like the snail had been.

But the cat remained.

Ember noticed its eyes. They were different colours. One was red and one was blue.

'You shouldn't be here,' it said to her. 'Not yet. I've come to take you back.'

With everything else that had happened this afternoon she felt she shouldn't have been too surprised by a talking cat, but she was.

'Oh,' she said.

'It's a cat,' said Ness.

'Yes,' Ember said. And then she said, 'I saw you before,' to the cat.

'I saw you too,' said the cat. 'I didn't like that man. So I followed.'

'He left me here,' Ember said. 'Wherever here is. Is this heaven?'

The cat looked at her. And blinked.

'It's just a place that happens to the dead,' it said after a pause.

'Are you dead?' Ember asked.

'I'm a cat,' the cat said.

'Am I dead?' she asked.

'No,' it replied.

Happiness didn't say anything. That wasn't like her.

There was a whistling out in the street and the woman in the bright dress, its colours a startling fresh tang in the grey world, was walking towards them.

'You,' she said, 'shoo.'

She waved her hands and the cat jumped down from the wall, on the opposite side to the girls, so they never saw where it went.

'You can't stay here,' the woman said, walking up the path and looking at December. 'I've thought about it and I've made a decision. The deal is off. I'm going to give you back.'

'Back?'

'To where you belong. Not here. Back to your own people.'

'Oh,' said Ember.

'Just come with me. It won't take a second. We'll go the short way.'

She held her hand out for December to take.

'But what about …' Ember said, looking at Ness, who was still sat on the doorstep.

'It stays here,' the woman said.

'I won't go without her,' Ember said.

Happiness looked at her, blinking as if she was staring at a bright light, and then she looked down, having said nothing.

'It won't be here for long,' said the woman. 'Dust on the wind soon.'

'No,' shouted Ember. She hated hearing people talk like this, talk as if nothing could be changed, as if bad things were just things that happened, as if her friend didn't count for anything, as if she were an 'it' and not a 'she'. She hated this woman, whose dress was so colourful and whose smile was so warm, in this world of grey and shadow and silence.

She spun round and pointed at the woman, fire in her veins.

'No! I won't leave her behind. I won't leave her on her own in this horrible place. Bring her with us. Take her home. You've got to –'

'I *have* to do nothing,' the woman snapped, her voice become thunder. 'You *cannot* command me.' Then she softened.

Shook her head. Breathed. 'Don't you realise, girl, I'm doing something good for you?' She laid her hand on Ember's upper arm. Her touch was ice cold and iron strong. 'People have offered me fortunes and lives and empires to do this for them. But you get this one for free because I'm Just.'

Before Ember could say,

'Just what?'

she felt a lurch in her stomach and a sensation all over her body like diving into cold water, or rather, like diving through cold water and then she was dry and warm and dry was she again and as she looked around her she was stood exactly where she had been stood, in Ness's front garden, except birds were singing and the grass was green and the sky was a hundred shades of red where a fat, dull orange sun was sinking.

And Ness was gone.

The doorstep was empty.

'Ember? Ember!'

It was her dad's voice.

He was in the front garden next door, in their own front garden.

'Where have you been? We've been worried sick. We've phoned everyone and no one knew where you were. I've been out looking. Penny's out on her bike, trawling the streets right now.'

The woman let go of her arm, turned to face Ember's dad, and smiled.

'I spotted her wandering near the park,' she said. 'I brought her home for you.'

'Who are you?'

'Ms Todd. I work for Social Services.' She handed Harry a card that she produced from the air. 'I'm at the school for the next few days, in case any children need to talk about what happened. I'm there to listen. To support. You know.'

She smiled and leant her head to one side.

'Oh, of course.'

Harry looked at the card. Read it. Seemed to be satisfied with what it said.

Ember said nothing, looking from one grown-up to the other.

She was trying to decide if this story was better than the real one. Which would get her into more trouble?

Her heart skipped strangely inside her chest. Happiness was in her head.

'It's perfectly natural that some of the children are upset, want to seek out a little solitude, a little time of their own. This one wandered. I thought it safest I brought her home.'

'Thank you, Ms Todd,' Harry said. 'But that's the wrong house.'

Ms Todd laughed and said, 'I see that now. I guess we're all a bit absent-minded today, aren't we?'

That evening, after Ember had had a bath and once she was sat up in bed, her dad came and sat on the floor beside her.

'You know you can talk to me,' he said. 'You can talk to me about anything. Anything that's on your mind.'

She nodded.

'And you know I'm not mad, I'm not angry, but I was just so worried when you didn't come home. December, darling, don't ever do that to me again. Promise me? Penny was so worried. You know that she loves you too, don't you?'

She nodded.

Of course she knew that.

When December woke she lay in bed, making a list of new things she knew, or thought she knew.

She traced them out on the ceiling.

Firstly, the dead *sort of* don't die. There's a place where they live on for a bit. It's boring and grey and silent and she didn't want to go back there.

Secondly, her mum's brother, Uncle Graham, had made some sort of 'deal' with that Ms Todd person to get Betty back from that place. It seemed like he'd *swapped* Ember for Betty. A live girl for a dead dog.

Thirdly, Ms Todd said that she'd changed her mind about the deal. Ms Todd had brought her back from that black and white world just by touching her arm. She clearly wasn't a normal grown-up.

Fourthly, last night Harry had told her that even Uncle Graham had been out looking for her. But Uncle Graham had known full well where she was when she was missing.

Fifthly, she'd not told Harry and Penny that Uncle Graham had swapped her, in the world of the dead, for his dog. Partly because they wouldn't have believed her, but also because there'd've been all sorts of fuss. She hadn't *exactly* gone off with a stranger, but still …

Sixthly (or fifth-and-a-halfly), she hadn't needed to get her uncle in trouble because she wanted to talk to him. She wanted him to tell her how he'd made this 'deal' with Ms Todd.

And seventhly, and every-other-numberthly, Happiness was still there, in that other place, and Ember missed her, wanted her back. The world was too quiet without her.

She went to school as usual.

Harry walked with her, but she didn't listen to what he was saying because she was making plans in her head. There were so many things she wanted to do and they all rolled around inside her like kittens in a washing machine. Every now and then she'd see a little face pressed up against the glass and it made sense, but mostly it was just a jumble.

'You promise me?' her dad said.

'What?'

'Have you been listening to a word I've been saying?'

'I was thinking.'

'Just like your mum,' he said. 'Off in your own world.'

He ruffled her hair.

They were at the school gates.

'I said,' he said, '"Make sure you come straight home after school." That's all. Or do you want me to come and pick you up? Or Penny could?'

She thought for a moment.

'I'll be fine,' she said. 'Straight home after school. I promise.'

'I love you, Ember,' he said and kissed the top of her head.

'Harry!' she said, feeling shocked and looking round to check whether anyone had seen.

She ran off through the gates and up the path to the playground.

School went ahead.

They learnt some more about Vikings.

They were making a longboat to go on the wall.

She spent the class before break making shields out of tin foil and paper and glue, to go on the side of the ship, but she was thinking about other things as she cut and shaped and stuck.

She was buzzing with secrets. There was no one she could talk to, though, no one she could tell. Her classmates would think her bonkers. Even Vincent, who'd once seen a ghost, would look at her weirdly, and her teachers would think she was just upset and confused because of … because of what had happened. Oh! She needed Happiness there. She was the only one who would've understood, who would've been as excited as Ember.

At break they were all let out on to the playground. The field was too wet still, after the recent rain, and they weren't allowed on it.

Nevertheless, when Amanda was knocked over by a football she was trying to head and everyone rushed round her on the tarmac, Ember slipped past the side of the school building and on to the field.

It wasn't very muddy at all.

Her heart was banging against her ribs, like a bird trying to escape a cat.

She'd never done anything like this before.

She ran, half tiptoeing, half skipping, across the grass, until she reached the row of trees that split the field in two.

She leant her back against the first one she came to, the school out of sight behind her, and tried to get her breath back.

Oh gosh.

Was she really doing this?

She could imagine the trouble she'd be in when everyone went in from break and they realised that she wasn't there.

She'd never done anything like this before.

Miss Short would go crazy. She'd probably phone Harry, and he'd go crazy too.

But later, when they all saw what she'd done (if she did what she hoped to do), then all the trouble in the world, and more, would be worth it.

With her heart still flapping wildly, but her breathing a little more under control, she ran across the field to where the chain-link fence was loose and slipped under it, out into the street.

From there it was only five minutes' walk, past the newsagent's and past the bakery (the window filled with doughnuts and pastries and coconut slices), past the buses and parked cars and the people out walking dogs or pushing shopping trolleys or talking to the postman (they looked at her as she went by, but she ignored them, trying to look like a girl who had been allowed out of school for a special reason, and not like a truant), to Uncle Graham's house.

She'd never done anything like this before.

His motorbike was parked on the street.

The pannier in which he carried organs from hospital to hospital glowed.

The whole world glowed. So alive.

She rang the doorbell.

Inside there was silence, and then thunking and a crash, and then footsteps, and then the door opened a crack.

'Yes?'

A sliver of Uncle Graham's face appeared in between the door and the frame.

The eye she could see was red and veiny, as if he had been up too late.

It took him a moment to recognise her.

'*You*?' he said.

He turned pale, missed a breath and stepped backwards.

The door swung open a little wider.

'No,' he said. 'You're … You can't be …'

She was sure that Harry had phoned him the evening before to say that she'd come home, but maybe Uncle Graham hadn't been listening properly, or maybe he'd somehow forgotten.

He was slowly swaying as he stood there, at the foot of the stairs, staring at her as if he had been punched a knockout blow by a huge boxer.

She pushed the door open and stepped into the hall.

A purpose was in her heart.

She wasn't afraid and she wasn't uncertain.

He stepped back.

'Tell me how to do it,' she said.

'What? Do what?'

He held on to the newel post as he spoke, but his eyes were

shuffling their feet nervously, as if really he was scared, cornered, confused. He seemed smaller than she'd ever seen him before, even though he was the same size as ever.

'Bring her back.'

His mouth hung open and he didn't say anything for a moment.

'How did you … ?' he asked eventually.

'Never you mind,' she said. 'If you don't show me how to bring Happiness back from the dead, then I'll tell Harry what you did.'

'You what?'

'You heard. I'll tell him you brought me back here after school and that you knew where I was all along … You knew where I was when they were all looking for me.'

She didn't mention the other thing he'd done, the worse thing, the thing no one would believe, but she saw it fly across his face anyway.

He stepped backwards, half staggering as if he wanted to put more space between them.

'Oh,' he said.

And suddenly he began crying.

Little sobs that caught in his throat.

He wiped his nose on his arm.

The hair glistened like a snail trail.

Seeing him like this was the first thing that wobbled Ember's resolve. She hadn't expected him to cry. She'd just expected him to help.

This man who raced round the country on his motorbike, saving lives, delivering the heart or the kidneys in the nick of time for the operation that would give someone a second chance ... she hadn't expected him to break down. He was a grown-up. Grown-ups weren't supposed to cry.

He slumped down on to the stairs, and sat on the bottom step looking past her and weeping.

She went into the front room to look for a box of tissues or a hankie or something to give to him, but she didn't find a box of tissues.

She stopped in the doorway.

There, beside the gas fire, was Betty's dog basket, and in it was Betty, and she wasn't moving.

She was in colour now, like a real live dog, but she wasn't moving.

Ember tiptoed closer.

It didn't look like the dog was breathing. The ribcage wasn't going up and down or anything.

'Amber, don't ...'

Her not-quite-name rippled out of the hallway between sniffs and snurfs, and lingered in the front room like a raised hand.

Looking back she could see Graham on the stairs, through the banisters. He was looking at her, looking at Betty.

She turned back.

Betty was dead. Dead again.

He'd brought her back from wherever that place was, from the black and white world, from the underworld, the afterworld, only for her to die again.

But then she thought about Ms Todd, big and bright and brutal, and of how she had said the deal was off. How she had brought Ember back when Ember should have been left there. He'd *swapped* her life for Betty's, hadn't he? That *had* been what he'd done, hadn't it?

So when she came back, the re-alived Betty must've died again. Was that how it had worked? (She saw a see-saw in her mind, one end raised up in the world of the living, one dipped down in the world of the dead. A set of scales having to balance one side with the other.)

She'd never liked Betty, but knowing that she'd snatched away the dog's new life made her feel like a cheat for a moment, made her feel like it was *she* who'd done something wrong.

She laid a hand on the dog's side.

It was cold.

It wasn't breathing.

It felt like the threadbare stuffed fox that the kids dared each other to touch whenever there was a school trip to the town museum.

But then the head swung up and looked at her with milky

white eyes and the jaw lolled open, hanging down from the head like that of a broken puppet, and a noise like a gurgling bark, a woof lost underwater and far away, crumpled out of the mouth and fell to the carpet.

December leapt back as Betty staggered to her feet, unsteady and leaning, and then slumped into her basket, grumpling and gurgling.

Drool drippled on to the tartan blanket, and then she was still again.

Ember felt sick but was pinned in place.

She didn't want to turn round, didn't want to look away from Betty, in case she moved again. But she could feel Graham's eyes watching her from behind. They tickled like cold and long-nailed fingers.

'She was fine,' he said. 'Fine when we came back. Just like ever, Amber. She was perfect again. And then … something changed.' He paused. Sums added up in his head. Gears crunched sand and dust as they rolled together. Then he spoke again. 'You,' he said. 'You've come back. She said …' But he trailed off again and never said what she'd said, or who the 'she' who'd said it had been.

Betty hadn't moved since that strange, lolling lunge, so December dared to turn her back.

Graham was on the second from bottom step of the stairs, wiping his nose on one arm, drying his cheeks with the other, and staring at her through the doorway.

He was no longer the slumped-in-sorrow ex-dog owner he'd been a minute before; now he had become something else. He had become, she saw, a man who'd found someone to blame.

What had seemed like a good idea at the time, a crazy but overwhelming idea, now felt like a mistake.

She would do *anything* to bring Ness back, of course she would, but asking Uncle Graham how he'd done it had not been the right move. Why did she ever imagine *he* would help *her*? He'd been willing to leave her *there* for the sake of an ugly old dog. Why would he suddenly help? He didn't even know her right name.

And now he was starting to get up, to heave himself up.

He was bigger than she was, and now he hated her. A black spark had sprung up in his chest. The dog he had worked some magic to save, *she* had taken from him. She didn't think he would forgive her.

A dark fire in his brain, twisting like a worm.

Her only hope was to dodge him, to outrun him.

As she thought this she was surprised to find that she was already darting past him down the hallway.

He was between her and the front door, so she was heading to the back.

Into the kitchen.

She skirted the big wooden table and slammed into the

back door, rattling the handle.

It turned easily, but the door was locked.

She looked around for a key.

It wasn't in the keyhole. It wasn't on the side. It wasn't on the table.

'Amber!'

He wasn't rushing.

He knew she was trapped.

He walked slowly along the passage.

She could feel his eyes on her.

There was a scrabbling sound too, and a thin whining, as if something else were coming towards her as well.

And then … there it was!

Hanging on a hook to one side, near the top of the back door, was the key that would let her out.

It was beyond her reach, and even when she jumped for it her fingertips only just brushed it, barely nudged it, set it wobbling.

Gasping, she tugged a chair out from under the table and climbed up on it, putting a hand on the work surface beside her to keep her balance.

She hooked the key down, but paused as she felt what her other hand was touching.

It was a sheet of paper, folded and folded again.

It was cold to the touch, in just the way paper never usually was.

'Amber, we need to talk,' Graham said as he stepped into the kitchen.

'No,' she said simply, without listening to herself.

She risked turning her back on him just long enough to get the key in the keyhole.

Her hands were shaking and it took go after go to do, but then, at last, it was in.

As she turned it, she glanced over her shoulder.

Graham was looking away from her. Looking down and behind him.

In the dark of the hallway, back there, Betty was staggering after her master, short and dribbly and whimpering.

The lock clicked and she pulled the door open.

She knocked the chair over on her way out and slammed the door behind her.

She ran through the scrubby little garden and yanked open the back gate.

Out into the alley and off to the right.

She risked pausing for a second, leant on her knees and took several deep breaths.

She was surprised to find that she still had the key in her hand. She shoved it in her pocket.

Oh! Why had she left school? Why had she run away? She

was going to be in so much trouble.

She heard the back door opening, and although she couldn't make out the words, she heard Graham shouting for her.

She ran.

Down the alley and left at the junction.

The more corners she could put between them, the happier she'd be.

Another junction and left again.

And on, and again.

And then she slowed down.

There weren't supposed to be *any* junctions in the alley. Not in the *real* alley. It ran straight out to the road.

The folded sheet of paper in her hand shivered.

She looked down at it, surprised.

She didn't remember picking it up.

It was most odd.

She unfolded it.

Before it had felt cold to the touch, and it felt colder now.

It was a map. Or, at least, sort of.

There was an odd square spiral shape in the middle and writing she couldn't read round the outside.

The ink it was written in was black. Blacker than any ink she'd seen before, which was, she realised as soon as she'd thought it, a really odd thing to think. Black was black. But still …

As she looked, the spiral seemed to revolve, to go round, but it wasn't moving.

Obviously an optical illusion, she thought. Harry had shown her them on the internet. It wasn't anything unnatural, but that knowledge didn't slow her heart down.

She couldn't hear anyone behind her in the alley. Maybe she'd lost Graham; maybe he'd been left behind somewhere where there weren't any junctions.

She must be somewhere in between, she thought as she slowly walked forward to the next junction, not quite *there* yet, but not quite *here* either.

'Somewhere you shouldn't be,' said a voice.

The cat was sat on the same dustbin she'd seen it on the day before.

'Go back,' it said.

'I can't,' she replied.

'Going on is not an option either,' the cat said. 'Not for you.'

'I need to save my friend,' she said. 'I need to go on.'

She walked past the cat. She'd come this far and she was right: she couldn't turn back. Wouldn't turn back.

Behind her the cat scratched at one of its tatty ears.

Blinked its odd-coloured eyes.

Stepped away and
v a n i s h e d.

She opened the gate and, as before, stepped into a world where all the colour had been washed away.

The alley was still bright behind her; sunlight fell on the fence opposite, turning it fiery green and brown and orange.

The garden before her was grey and grey and grey.

She stepped in and shut the gate.

She waited a moment, and then opened it again.

The alley wasn't grey.

She heard a bird singing somewhere out there.

This was still the door back to her world, back to the world of the living.

Maybe it stayed open until someone went through it?

Someone living?

Someone dead?

How could she know?

Yesterday the alley had become grey and cornerless only after Graham and Betty and Ms Todd had gone through the gate. When they'd left her behind.

She needed the black and white alley though, to get out to the black and white street.

She opened the gate again, just to check, and it was still colourful.

So she wasn't going to find Happiness by going that way, not this time. She turned back to the house.

It looked just like Uncle Graham's house.

She ducked under the washing line and walked up to the back door.

It was locked.

She folded the piece of paper, the strange, cold spiral-map that had opened the alleys, and tucked it in her trouser pocket. She pulled the key from her other pocket.

It fitted and the door opened easily.

Inside was dark.

It was still.

Dust.

Her nose tickled with the desire to sneeze.

She stepped in.

She tiptoed through the kitchen, which was more or less the same as the one she'd been in just minutes earlier, except ...

the table was different … smaller, in a different place. Were the cupboards arranged differently too? It was hard to tell. She'd only ever seen the room a couple of times.

She went through into the passage and down to the hall.

On her left the stairs went up into darkness.

Shadows flickered between the bannisters.

On her right the door to the front room was ajar.

She remembered Betty's basket in there, back in the real world. She remembered it being empty, and she remembered it being full …

With shaking fingers she twisted the latch on the front door and opened it.

Out there was the grey street she'd hoped for.

She looked around in the hall for something to block the door with. She couldn't let it click shut after her or she'd never get back in, and as far as she knew the only way back to life was out the back gate …

There was an umbrella stand full of walking sticks that she was sure hadn't been there in Uncle Graham's house, but which felt solid and real enough when she touched it. (So whose house was this?)

She pulled a bundle of sticks and umbrellas out and laid them in the doorway so the door could swing to but couldn't close.

She just had to hope no one came along to tidy things up.

As she pulled the door open and lifted her leg to climb over the brollies, she heard a noise.

It came from the front room, from just behind the half-open door, from that room where the dog had been.

But it hadn't sounded like a dog. Not a bark or a woof or a yelp.

It had sounded more like a chair moving, or maybe someone moving in a chair. Springs and creaking. A sigh. A breath of some sort. And now her ears were open, she realised there'd been a low buzz, a hum, a rustle in the house all along. The atmosphere crackled faintly.

Whose house was this?

When the creaking, shifting sound didn't come again, she hopped over the sticks as quietly as she could and, not daring to look over her shoulder, walked on.

And so, out into the street.

And so, out into the world.

And so.

12

The silence of the world smothered her. No bird sang, no car roared, no voice laughed.

Even her footsteps were dulled, softened, hushed.

Whenever she looked behind her, there was no one there. Just the black and white and empty reflection of the world she knew.

Passing the school, she looked at the playground.

She and Happiness had run around there like idiots, arms out like fighter planes, shooting each other down, before falling in a heap and laughing. So many times. So often. So simple.

That was what she remembered most. Laughter.

They sometimes laughed until they cried, not always at anything particularly funny, just *because*.

She hurried on.

Happiness was sat on the doorstep where December had left her the day before.

She covered her eyes with the back of her hand as she looked up, as if she were blocking out the sun on a summer's day.

'Deck?' she said.

Her voice was flat, quiet.

'Yes, it's me. I've come to rescue you.'

Ness lowered her hand. Looked away.

'I didn't think you'd come back. That woman …'

Woman?

'Ms Todd?' Ember said.

'I don't know her name. The one who took you away just now.'

Just now?

'Just now?' Ember said.

Ness looked confused.

'It was just now, wasn't it?

Or was it years ago?

I don't know.

I feel so odd.

Like I'm not myself,

like I'm asleep

or falling asleep.

And then I look up and the sun hasn't moved. Nothing's happened.'

Ember looked behind her, over to the houses on the opposite side of the road where she'd seen the black sun setting the day before. And there it was, round and black like a hole in the sky, exactly where it had been before. It hadn't moved, had it?

And as she looked at the sun, she was startled by a movement. Not in the sky, but in the house below.

A curtain twitched.

A net curtain in an upstairs window moved to one side and she saw a face looking out.

The curtain fell back again and the face was gone.

'Mrs Miłosz,' Ness whispered, having seen what Ember had seen. 'She scares me. She looks at me. Watches me. And I've got nowhere to go.'

Mrs Miłosz was an old lady who had lived opposite the girls until the previous summer. She'd fallen down the stairs and the district nurse had found her. Ember remembered the ambulance. She'd never seen one in her street before. It had been exciting – the flashing lights, the colours, the sheer boldness of the thing sitting there on her street.

Mrs Miłosz's sons had come and cleared the house with a big van the following week and a new family moved in a few weeks after that and soon the whole affair had been forgotten.

Ember was silent for a moment, spiders crawling across her skin.

'The woman?' she asked. 'You were saying something about Ms Todd.'

'She said you wouldn't be back,' Ness said. 'She said I was to forget you, that I was to forget everything. She told me not to hope. "Don't hope any more," she said.'

'Well, ignore her. Forget about *her* instead,' Ember said. 'She was wrong. I found a way and I've come to take you back. To take you back home.'

She explained, as quickly as she could, trying to make it make sense in her head as she said it, about the deal Uncle Graham had made. Explained how he'd swapped her for Betty – how leaving a live person behind had let him take a dead one back. 'But,' she added quietly, 'the important thing is he found a way to here, from there. And the gate's open now, it's open back to the real world. I checked. There's still sunlight and colour out there. If we both go through it together, then we'll be in the alleys and we can go home. Nothing can go wrong.' She added that last bit, not because she believed it (she was being careful not to believe in anything too much) but to sound confident for Ness.

She put her hand out, ready to haul her friend to her feet.

'Come on,' she said.

Ness had nodded as Ember had talked, but she didn't seem excited, didn't seem to want to do anything but sit down.

'I don't know,' she said eventually, with something like a sigh.

'Maybe I should just stay here.'

Oh. It was as if when all the colour had been drained from her, all the energy had gone too, all the spark that used to be there. The Ness Ember knew would've jumped to her feet, would've shouted an enormous 'Yes!' to the sky, would've been the first one to make an adventure of it.

(Was she greyer now? Flatter than the first time they'd met here? Ember didn't want to think about it too hard. Sometimes if you asked questions you learnt the answers, and answers aren't always good things to hear.)

Being dead had changed her, and knowing that meant that Ember forgave her. She was sure, she hoped, that going back to the world of the living, getting some colour back into her, taking her back to her mum and dad would bring the old Ness back. She didn't doubt that the old Ness was just hiding, was just underneath the grey, but knowing that, and forgiving her, couldn't stop the frustration bubbling up.

'I bunked off school to bring you back from the dead,' she said, louder and sharper than she'd intended. 'I'm gonna be in *so much* trouble if I don't bring you back.'

She really didn't mean to snap, really didn't want to sound (or be) angry with her friend, but *something* needed doing.

'Come on,' she said, getting her hand round Ness's wrist and pulling her to her feet.

Ness said nothing, but stood up, shaking her wrist free and rubbing at it.

'Sorry,' she said. 'That hurt.

It stung.

Burned.'

But still she followed Ember

up

the

crazy-paving

path

and

out

on

to

the

pavement.

Friends, still.

As they walked through the familiar but alien-looking streets, Ember tried to keep a stream of jolly chat going. *It's what you do when your friend's feeling down, isn't it?* she told herself. But it was hard because Ness didn't join in.

'So Harry said,' she continued, 'that I can have a phone for my next birthday and I'm worried he's gonna get me one of those pink ones with sparkles and stickers that you can use to individualise it for yourself. But I just want one that works and doesn't look stupid, but he still reckons I'm a little girl and that I want everything to be pink all the time …' This wasn't true. Harry didn't think that and she knew it and felt bad saying it, but she had to say something.

Ness just nodded, and said, 'Oh yes?' every now and then, but she wasn't coming up with any stories of her own. She wasn't making an effort to help Ember out.

She was blunted.

'So there was this programme on telly last night,' Ember tried, 'about this bloke who collected the labels from soup cans. Not soup cans themselves, just the labels, and he got arrested in the supermarket once for peeling the label off a can he'd never seen before when he didn't have enough money to buy it, and then when the soup company heard about it they sent him a whole box of tins of soup because it had been such good publicity for them, but the thing was he hated soup, couldn't stand the stuff, so he took the labels off and gave the tins away to the local food bank. He wrote the flavours on in marker pen, because he wasn't stupid, but they wouldn't take them because of health and safety, even though there were people who could've really done with some soup. But you can't go round giving out tins of soup with the names written on in marker pen because … well, you can't really trust a bloke who goes round writing on tin cans with a marker pen, can you?'

'Suppose not,' said Ness.

They'd long passed the school and were now about to turn into the road where Uncle Graham lived.

At the corner, Ember stopped walking.

She tugged at Ness's sleeve and stopped her too. (She was careful to not touch her this time.)

'What is it?'

'Look,' said Ember.

'It's that woman,' said Ness, turning away.

There, halfway down the road, outside the house they were aiming for, was Ms Todd. Her summer dress flapped in the breezeless air, bright and colourful and dazzling after the grey, grey, grey of the town.

She wasn't looking their way, so Ember quickly, without thinking, dragged Ness into someone's front garden.

They ducked down behind the low wall.

Grey flowers grew in neat little flowerbeds, poking up from the grey earth, surrounding a grey lawn.

'She said I shouldn't hope,' Ness said, almost to herself.

'There's always hope,' Ember replied. 'I didn't think there was hope when Mr Dedman said your name in assembly the other day, but then look what happened … look where we are. We're together again and I didn't think to even hope for that, it was such a mad idea, but here we are. Sometimes hope turns up when you least expect it.'

'When did you get so wise, Deck?' Ness said, reaching up and almost touching Ember's cheek with her grey fingers.

It was a strange gesture, not one Happiness had ever done before, not when she'd been alive. It was the sort of thing a mother would do, the sort of thing someone sad and saying goodbye might do.

'Dunno,' Ember said, answering the question. 'I just did what I had to do.'

She poked her head out and snuck a glance up the road.

'Has she gone?' whispered Ness.

'I can't see her,' said Ember. 'She's not in the street any more, so yeah, maybe.'

The two girls, the one full of colour and blood and light and nerves, the other washed out and black and white and made of grey, crept up the road, keeping close to the walls of the front gardens.

'It's this one,' Ember said as they reached the house.

The front door was still wedged open, just how she'd left it. All they had to do was go through the house and out the back gate.

It was easy.

So easy.

'We're almost there,' she said, smiling to herself.

'I can't,' said Ness.

She didn't move when Ember pulled her sleeve. She remained glued to the pavement.

'Come on.'

'I can't.'

Ember took a deep breath.

Don't get angry, she thought. *Don't be mad.*

'Look, I know you're nervous,' she said. 'You're probably worried about what we'll say to your mum and dad. But forget that. They'll just be so happy to have you back. They won't even ask any questions.'

'It's not that,' said Ness.

She couldn't take her eyes off the house.

'What are you looking at?' Ember asked.

She was beginning to worry.

She tugged her friend's sleeve again and still she wouldn't move.

'There's something in there.'

Ember looked at the house.

'Ms Todd?'

'Something else,' whispered Ness. 'Her, maybe, but something else too. Something worse.'

Ember thought about what she'd heard as she'd passed through half an hour earlier. What *had* she heard?

'It doesn't matter,' she said. 'We'll just run through. It'll take five seconds. The back door's open.'

And then the front door opened and Ms Todd was there. She was looking over her shoulder, back into the house, as if she were talking to someone.

She bent down to pick up the umbrellas and sticks that blocked the door and she saw the girls.

A strange look crossed her face. Amusement, perhaps? Weariness, maybe?

'You again,' she said, looking Ember straight in the eyes.

'Yes, me again,' said Ember, puffing up tall.

'I did you a favour last time,' Ms Todd said. 'I sent you home, despite the paperwork, despite the promises made. Because it was the *right thing to do*. A *dog*, for *you*? No!' She shook her head, almost laughing. An angry, disbelieving, narrow little laugh. 'It would serve you right if I left you this time. *This time* you've got no one else to blame, have you? This time it was *your* doing, *your* idea.

But still, young lady, I'm not ready for you. You're not ready for this. Not ready for here. Not ready for "Goodbye". I am Pity. I am Forgiveness. I am Kind.'

Ms Todd stepped forward, tall and awful, her movements smooth and relentless, like a train clearing the platform.

Ember ran, a sudden wordless cry in her chest urging her on, urging her to get away. Away!

In her panic she knocked Ness over and tumbled across the tarmac herself, before she scrambled to her feet and fled up the road.

She didn't get far before the strong grip of Ms Todd's hand fell on her shoulder.

'December, my dear girl,' the woman said, her breath cold in Ember's ear as she struggled to get free, 'there's nothing you can do to beat me. Listen. It's *not my fault.*'

They plunged together through the water that wasn't there as the worlds changed.

There was the hoot of a car's horn and the sound of brakes.

Ember was thrown to the pavement, rolling in the sure protection of Ms Todd's embrace, out of the path of a staggeringly green car.

It hooted its horn again and screeched off.

'Are you all right?' someone was asking.

'Yes, we're fine, thanks,' Ms Todd was saying. 'These crazy

drivers come out of nowhere without looking. You've got to be so careful these days.'

Ms Todd delivered Ember back to school.

'Out for a dentist's visit,' she explained to Mrs Holland on reception.

'Oh yes, of course,' the woman said. 'How silly of us. We were worried sick. We tried calling your dad but haven't been able to get hold of him. Thought you'd run off.' She giggled a silly, high-pitched little giggle. 'You'd best get back to class, December, it's almost lunchtime.'

Mrs Holland didn't even ask who Ms Todd was. She didn't even seem quite to look at her. But her words had worked. Ember wasn't even in trouble.

She might not be in trouble, she thought, but she wasn't done yet.

She still had the magic map thing in one pocket, and Uncle Graham's back door key in the other.

Despite Ms Todd, she'd keep trying until she'd brought Happiness back.

Ember wasn't about to give up on her friend.

Not yet.

     Not now.

          Not ever.

The rest of the day went by slowly.

There was a bubble of excitement in her chest that she fought to contain.

Everyone else was still quiet and Happiness's death still echoed in the school, dulling everything. And it echoed most especially in the classroom they'd shared. There was an empty space on their table and the poem Ness had written about Easter was still on the display board. (They'd all written poems, but only the best ones had been pinned up.)

December wanted to stand up and shout, 'She'll be back soon! Tomorrow, she'll be back here! I promise!' but she didn't.

When she got home that afternoon, Penny let her in.

'You OK? Nice day at school?'

'Where's Harry?'

'He's had to go see a client,' she said. 'A last minute thing, but he should be home before you're in bed. You've got me cooking you tea. I hope you don't mind?'

She didn't mind. The only thing that Penny could cook was hot dogs, the sort you boil for four minutes. Anything that required more complicated cooking than that became inedible. Ember liked hot dogs.

While Penny got the water on to boil, Ember chopped an onion and put some oil in the little frying pan.

'You be careful with that,' Penny said.

There was a broken pair of old dark glasses in the kitchen drawer (they only had one arm) and Ember put them on to stop the oil from spitting in her eye.

'Safety first,' she said, dropping the shredded onion into the pan.

The sizzling was lovely, the smell mouthwatering and the hot dogs slightly overboiled, though you hardly cared once you hid them under ketchup (not mustard) and onions and swaddled them in soft white rolls.

It was only once they'd finished their tea and had wiped their hands and mouths and Ember had swapped her now rather food-stained school shirt for a clean T-shirt that she noticed the card half hidden under a pile of half-opened post on the sideboard.

It looked like an invitation, the sort of card you got from a friend telling you about a birthday party, saying what time and where and whether it was fancy dress or not. Except it was colourless. It was white and silver and simple and had the date of Happiness's funeral in it. The following Monday. It was Thursday evening now. She needed to get Happiness back before then, she thought. Even though she knew a funeral wouldn't make Ness any *more* dead, for some reason it felt like a deadline to her.

December was sat on her bed in her dressing gown, drying her hair with a towel. She'd just had her bath and other than the bathroom, which still rolled steamy air out on to the landing, the house was cold. Harry said it was immoral to have the heating on at this time of year.

There was a banging on the front door.

She jumped when she heard it.

She glanced at the window. It was already getting dark outside. Why didn't they ring the bell?

Bang.

Bang.

Bang.

She heard her dad stacking plates in the kitchen. He'd come

home while she was in the bath and had shouted a hello through the door, but she'd not seen him yet.

His footsteps crossed the hall as she scooted herself across the bed to look out at the street.

She could hear raised voices in the hall, someone shouting words she couldn't quite make out and Harry answering in a quieter, kinder voice. What was that all about?

She pressed her face to the glass and tried to see down.

She couldn't see who it was at the door, but there was something in the garden, something low and squat and animal-like moving around in the shadows by the front wall. It staggered as if it were uncertain on its feet. The shrubs and flowers shuddered as it banged into them, like a lamb climbing up on to all four legs for the first time.

And then she looked up and she saw the house across the road. The lights were on upstairs and the woman who lived there, a young woman with a baby and a boyfriend and two cats, looked out at her from the window of the big bedroom. Ember thought she smiled as she drew the curtains. And Ember remembered old Mrs Miłosz, who'd lived there before. Then she heard the front door slam and she looked back down to the garden and saw Uncle Graham walk away, and poor, pitiable, not-alive Betty fell out of the shadows after him, limping and hobbling and trailing grimness behind her.

Graham leant on the wall as he went out on to the pavement. He glanced up at the front of the house, and his red eyes roved across it.

She ducked backwards, falling flat on her bed with a bounce.

Had he seen her?

She knew she didn't want him to know she'd seen him, didn't want him to know she'd been watching.

And then there was a soft knock at her door.

'Ember, you decent?' Harry asked.

She sat up and pulled her dressing gown around her.

'Yeah,' she said.

Harry opened the door, came in, sat on the floor by the bed.

'The weirdest thing just happened,' he said. 'Did you hear?'

'Uncle Graham?' she asked. 'I saw him out the window.'

'Yes. Did you hear what he said?'

'No.'

'The poor man,' Harry said. 'He was raving. He must have been drinking. I don't think I've ever seen him drunk before. It's so sad, what some people become. What sadness does to them.'

'What did he say? He sounded angry …'

'Oh, you mustn't pay any attention to him, love. He's upset. He loved his Betty like she was his best friend. I don't think that he has many friends. Your mum said he was a lonely one, even back when they were kids. They grew up in that house of his, you know.'

While your mum went off travelling and partying and loving the world, he stayed behind looking after their parents and tinkering with his motorbikes.'

It was nice to hear about her mum. Ember imagined her young and dancing on some tropical beach, flowers in her hair and the white crests of waves crashing on to the sand behind her. She was lovely, and suddenly Ember missed her in a way she'd not done for a long time. She missed her like she missed Happiness.

'He went on about how Betty won't stop following him about. Won't leave him alone. How she's alive and dead and alive again. Weird stuff. I think poor Betty being knocked down's knocked him for six. I hope he can find some help.' He put a big, warm hand on December's knee and looked up into her face. 'Look, you keep away from him for a bit, OK? If you bump into him, just give him a smile and then come home, OK?' He shook his head. 'I'm sure in the morning he'll have sobered up, and if he remembers what he said, he'll be dead embarrassed probably, but all the same ... Be safe, Ember. OK?'

She patted Harry's big, warm hand.

'Of course,' she said. 'Of course I'll be safe.'

Before she went to bed she unfolded the map on the desk where she did her homework.

It was cold, like it wasn't made of paper, but of metal or stone or something.

Looking at the spiral path's strange slow twist made her giddy.

On top of it she laid the key to Uncle Graham's back door.

The questions that she didn't know the answers to were:

Will the map lead me through the alleys, even if I don't start from Uncle Graham's house?

Does the map only work in that alley, or might it work somewhere else too?

Will Happiness be waiting where I last saw her, at Uncle Graham's house, or will she be back on her own front step?

(And the question she almost didn't dare to think: *How can I stop what happened to Betty from happening to Ness?*)

That last question she pushed to the back of her mind. Too terrifying. She'd not thought it, or had managed to ignore it when she'd tried to rescue Ness that morning, but the shadow of it had grown in her mind, the seriousness of it.

Despite that, somehow, eventually, thoughtlessly, sleep took her hand and sank with her into darkness and silence and peace.

·FOURTEEN·

In the middle of the night December woke up.

There'd been a noise on the stairs.

It was pitch black and she couldn't move.

She was lying on her side under the duvet and now there was something in the room and she couldn't move a muscle.

She strained and heaved but her limbs were like lead, like stone. She stared at the wall, at where she knew the wall was in the darkness. Her back was to the door, to the room, and something was moving towards her.

She could hear footsteps – quiet, tiptoeing – tiny footsteps, and she wanted to scream, wanted to shout for her dad, wanted to make a noise to let whoever it was know that she knew they were there, wanted to hurl the duvet off and make a noise and scare them away.

But she was frozen.

Her heart thumped.

She could feel tears tickling over the bridge of her nose.

Lead.

Stone.

A statue.

Paralysed.

Petrified.

And then something landed on the bed.

Thud!

Something had jumped up and landed on the bed, in the dark.

Something had sat down beside her.

And then something cold touched her forehead, touched her ear, touched her cheek.

Cold and wet.

And a voice said, 'I see you.'

Ember sat up in bed, in the dark, her knees tucked up under her chin and the duvet wrapped round her.

In the darkness she could just make out the shape of the cat in front of her.

As it moved its head its eyes glinted, damp and shining.

It spoke and she listened.

Its voice was kind, firm, honest, sharp, but reserved. A short distance away from being warm.

'I know what you're thinking,' it said.

'I can hear you across the town,' it said.

'No good will come of it,' it said.

'You can't do it,' it said.

'Things are the way they are,' it said.

It licked its paw and worried at its ear.

Although she couldn't see it now, she remembered the ragged look of the ear, the ragged look of the cat. As if it had been dragged backwards through a hedge, a ditch and a scrub of cacti and hadn't bothered to comb its hair afterwards.

She didn't think a little lick and brush of the ear would be enough.

'Things are the way they are *for a reason*?' she said, half asking a question.

The cat stopped washing.

'No,' it said, after a moment. 'No reason. They just are, and that's all there is to it. Some things you just have to accept and move on from.'

'But she didn't deserve to die,' Ember said.

'No,' said the cat. 'Few do. But she died, all the same.'

'But I've seen her. I can bring her back. Bring her back here.'

'You've not seen her,' said the cat. 'All you've seen are echoes. Just an echo. You think too much. You think *so* much. You people. I. I. I. *Me. Me. Me.* All the time. It rings in the world like a bell. It takes a while to fade away, that's all. *Cogitatis ergo estis.*'

'What does that mean?' she asked.

'It means it takes a while to forget that *you* were *you*.'

'That place … ?'

'It's where forgetting happens, that's all. Echoes. Echoes. Echoes. Your people echo longest, that's all. Nothing more.'

Ember thought of the snail she'd watched turn to dust and blow away.

'Snails?' she asked.

'Think very little of themselves,' said the cat immediately.

Hardly even know that they *are*. Only that they *do*. No self-reflection in a snail's mind.'

'Betty? The dog?'

'Dogs think of themselves more, yes. It's all: *Does he love me? Why can't I see him now? Have I upset him? When will he get here?* Awful things, all their thoughts tangled up in their humans.'

The cat looked away, licked its shoulder. Stopped licking.

Ember nodded. She thought she understood. Then she thought of a different question.

'And Ms Todd ... is she ... ?'

The cat said nothing, but jumped down from the bed.

It padded across the floor, its feet soft, its tail crooked in a sudden shaft of moonlight between the curtains.

'Do not do what you are going to do,' it said, as it reached the door. 'She isn't your friend, and I won't be there to help next time. I'm busy. I can hear mice, voles, rats ... Warm. Crunchy. Thinking of themselves just enough.'

December wondered who the 'she' was. Did the cat mean Ms Todd or Ness? Or both?

She sat there in silence, in the dark, long after the cat had gone, thinking.

Her dad got up.

She heard him banging into things and swearing softly as he made his way to the bathroom.

The toilet flushed.

On the way past her room he stuck his head round the door.

'Oh, Ember,' he said. 'Did I wake you up?'

'No,' she said. 'I was just thinking.'

'Always thinking,' he said. 'Just like her. So smart, so full of ideas. You don't get that from me.' He paused. 'She could've changed the world, you know. If she'd been given the chance. Changed it all round …'

He scratched at his pyjamas and came and sat on the floor beside the bed.

'Lie down,' he said. 'Shut your eyes.'

And, leaning on the mattress, with his fingers in her hair, he told her all about his day at work and the changes his client wanted made to the plans and how one sort of plasterboard is much better than another, but how, because it's more expensive, he was having a hard time making …

But by then she was asleep and dreaming of nothing.

Friday was a school day like the rest and December stayed in class, stayed at school all the way through.

She hadn't given up on Happiness though; it was just that now she had a better plan. Or a better start of a plan. Possibly. So long as she didn't look at it too closely.

That evening Harry and Penny were going out. They had tickets to the theatre to see a long play about people sat in a room arguing about who was in love with who. The play had been a hit a few years earlier, but this was the first time it had been put on nearby, so they'd jumped at the opportunity. The tickets had been pinned to the corkboard in the kitchen and the date had been circled on the calendar for ages.

Despite all that, Harry had sat down with her at breakfast and said, 'Ember, if you don't want us to go, we won't. If you want me to stay with you tonight, I will.'

He was a good man, she knew that, and he really wouldn't have minded if she'd said, 'Stay here.' He was really very sweet.

But, as it happened, she didn't want him to stay. Her plan needed him to go.

His mum and dad, Tilda and Porkpie, her gran and grandad, were going to be babysitting (even though she wasn't a baby), and that was going to give her all the opportunity she needed.

Tilda and Porkpie weren't like most grans and grandads she knew of.

They were old people made more like teenagers.

Ember wasn't sure what had gone wrong with them, but they'd failed to grow up properly.

After they'd hustled her upstairs ('I'll read for a bit, then go to bed,' she'd told them), they put popcorn in the microwave and snuggled up on the sofa to watch a movie they'd brought over.

Six months earlier Ember had come downstairs to get a glass of water or something, and had found them ignoring the movie entirely while cuddling and giggling and snogging. It had been absolutely horrible.

They hadn't noticed her and she'd snuck back upstairs, embarrassed, surprised and feeling ever so slightly sick.

It had been bad enough when she'd interrupted Harry and Penny, but at least they weren't *really old* and married and didn't smell of talcum powder, and at least they'd been *embarrassed*. Tilda and Porkpie had been together for *decades*, so quite why they were still so lovey-dovey she couldn't imagine, and she didn't want to ask. She just knew Porkpie would say something excruciating like, 'Phwoar, but I don't half fancy your gran something rotten, love,' because that was how he spoke. Embarrassingly.

But still she sort of liked them and they could be fun to go and stay with at Christmas, and, most importantly, they fitted perfectly with her plan for tonight.

Twenty minutes after they'd started their film, Ember slipped silently down the stairs, dressed and in her coat, and, under cover of
    explosions roaring out of the TV
    and kisses spilling from the settee,
    crept out of the front door,
    popping Harry's spare keys into her pocket.

She felt amazing.

Buzzing.

She walked through the streetlight-lit streets as if she did this
every evening.

Head up. Confident.

There were teenagers on bikes outside the newsagent's.

A bus passed by, an illuminated room gliding down the road.

The air was cold and there were a few speckles of rain in it.

She slipped into the alley behind Uncle Graham's house and
pulled the map from her pocket.

Was it going to work? Was just holding the map enough to make the corners appear for her to go round? Were there other rules?

She stood in the alley and it looked perfectly normal. A dead end at one end, the way out to the street at the other.

Even shutting her eyes and opening them again, even turning around and then turning back didn't change it.

The map chilled her skin, like holding a box of fish fingers straight from the freezer.

She turned the handle on Uncle Graham's gate. Maybe the map would only work its magic if she started from where she'd started before, from *that* back garden, by walking through *that* gate.

She pushed it open carefully and peered around.

The kitchen light wasn't on, but one of the upstairs lights was. A shadow was moving about in the room up there.

The garden was dark and she didn't think whoever was there (presumably her uncle, but you never knew) would see her, not if she was quick.

She took a couple of steps on to the mud that should've been a lawn and took a deep breath.

Pause.

Then she turned round and took a couple of steps back to the gate and went through it into the alley.

The map shivered in her hands like a kitten beginning to purr in its sleep.

She turned left and – yes! – ahead of her was the junction.

She ran round the corner, and then round the next one and the next, her heart keeping steady in the same way a girl walking a tightrope's does: arms wide, eyes shut.

As she passed the fourth corner she wondered where the cat was. It had normally seen her by now, normally made a comment of one sort or another. But not today.

In a way she felt relieved. It would only have tried to talk her out of this again. But at the same time she half missed it. It seemed to be on her side, more so than anyone else, even if it didn't agree with her plans.

But it wasn't there today.

Round the next corner and she pushed her uncle's gate open for the second time in a couple of minutes and there she was, back in the life-leeched black and white world. Dusty and drear.

It looked to be the same grey early evening it always was there.

She stepped from the darkening alley into thin, insipid daylight.

The back door was shut, but not locked this time. (Was that how she'd left it?)

As she tiptoed through the empty house she remembered, with a shiver, what Ness had said: 'There's something in there.'

The rustling, shifting sound she had heard before didn't come again. There was a faint crackle in the air, but all else was silence.

She hurried on.

She wedged the front door with the umbrellas and walking sticks, as before.

And she froze.

A bumblebee battered itself against the window of her chest.

She was filled with a sudden fear, a sudden flood of uncertainty.

Get Ness, she told herself. *Get Ness and get out of here.*

But, standing in the hallway, about to go out into the world, she felt like she was being watched.

The stairs reared up beside her. Was there someone up there?

And then – a noise from the front room.

Something shifting, something settling in place.

No footsteps.

No voice.

A humming, though, a hint of someone singing to themselves inside their head, and a faint, distant crackle in the air all around her.

Without turning to look, she jumped out into daylight, into the disappointing grey sunshine.

Ness wasn't in the front garden, wasn't waiting in the street for her, but nor was Ms Todd, so Ember turned left and headed off to their own houses.

Only once, walking those empty streets, did she see anything moving.

As she passed the school, something looped across the playing fields.

It was a squirrel, a dead squirrel, bouncing over towards the trees.

It saw her as she saw it and froze in place.

It looked at her, clutching its tail to its chest like an embarrassed woman with a handbag.

'Hello,' she said.

It didn't reply, but after having judged her to be no rival for ghost-nuts or phantom-acorns, or whatever squirrels ate in that dead world, it sprang off, bouncing across the field until it reached the tree, and wrapped itself around the trunk in spiralling loops, right up into the branches and out of sight.

So, she thought, *squirrels remember themselves longer than snails.* She didn't know what she would do with this information, but she stored it away, like an acorn.

What the scientists or psychologists would've given, she thought years later, looking back, to be able to come here and make a study of which animals hung around longest, which had the greatest dose of self-consciousness. But she wasn't a psychologist or a scientist … not yet.

Soon she was stood outside Happiness's house, yet again.

Happiness was back on her doorstep. Back in place. As if she'd never moved.

Did she look even fainter, even greyer, even more washed out than before? Maybe. Maybe.

It was hard to say. From the very first time December had found her here she'd been grey and washed out. Was she fading, or just waiting for a switch to flick from 'echoing' to 'silence'? The snail had been there, and then vanished – the robin too.

It was this place: it sucked the joy out of you.

Ember hoped that taking Ness back to the real world would fill her up with life and light and energy again. Everything that made Ness Ness.

'Deck?' Ness said quietly, without much surprise. 'I thought it was you.'

'I said I'd be back,' Ember said, and she found that her voice wobbled halfway through and the last word choked in her throat.

She felt her eyes growing misty.

'I said I'd come back,' she tried again.

'Thank you,' said Ness.

She stood up slowly, climbing to her feet like it was a great effort.

'We're going to have to be quick,' Ember said. 'We're going back the way we went before, but this time we won't get –'

'Won't get *what*?'

'– caught,' said Ember as she turned to look at Ms Todd.

'Ah,' said the woman.

She wasn't smiling any more.

'You shouldn't be here. I have warned you and saved you and sent you home and warned you again, but you insist on coming back.'

'Of course I keep coming back,' Ember said. 'How can I leave her here?' She pointed at Happiness. 'She's my best friend. This is what friends do.'

Ms Todd gave Ness barely a glance as she spoke.

'*It's* not anything. There are no *friends* here. This isn't that sort of place, December, my dear girl. That business is all over the moment you step through my gates.'

'No,' said Ember. She was bubbling inside, boiling like a kettle. 'No, that's not true. She's my friend … here, there and everywhere. *Anywhere. That* don't change.'

Ms Todd dismissed her with a wave of her hand.

'I can't be your protector any more. I'm busy. We are done. It's over. I'm sorry.'

She snapped her fingers, turned on her heel and strolled away up the street.

Ember shivered.

She'd been ignored, left as if she didn't matter.

It felt odd.

She felt odd.

Then she happened to look up, and across the street she saw the net curtain fall back into place as Mrs Miłosz stepped away from the window.

How long had she been watching? Ember wondered, and then she went to glance at her watch.

And she stopped.

Her heart stopped in her chest.

Her breath stopped in her throat.

Her mind stopped thinking; thoughts drifted to the ground like snow and lay unmoving around her feet.

Her watch, her wrist, her hand, her sleeve, her fingers were all drained of colour.

> She was black and white.
> She was shades of grey.
> She was like Ness.
> Like the world.
> She
> was
> dead.

'Oh, Deck, you're …' began Ness. Then she stopped.

Ember looked round and, for the first time in this bleached-out, leeched-out, black and white, not-right world, for the first time in the three visits she'd made here, Happiness was smiling.

It didn't matter what she'd been about to say. How she'd planned to finish the sentence she hadn't finished. Whether she'd been about to say 'dead' or 'black and white' or just 'like me', Ember recognised, and understood, that the sadness in the words was overcome, overwhelmed, by the fellowship, by the welcome, by the we're-together-again-ness of them.

She couldn't really, shouldn't really, blame Happiness for that, should she?

How lonely must she have been here all by herself?

Now they were together again.

Forever.

Or for as long as it took them to forget they'd ever been alive.

Dust on the wind, Ember thought. *Soon enough we'll be dust on the wind.*

But however much she understood Ness's words and her smile, she found it made her angry. Angry and sad.

She wanted to kick things. Wanted to break things. Wanted to shout the rudest words she knew at Ms Todd.

She wanted her dad.

Harry, where are you?

And she knew that if he knew about this place, he'd've been here in a shot, breaking down the walls between worlds, running through alleys, bursting through doors in order to rescue her. Just like she'd come to rescue Ness.

But he didn't know. There was no way he'd ever find her.

And then she wondered how it looked, back in the real world.

Ness had fallen off the swing. Someone had found her and they'd rushed her to hospital and she'd died, leaving a body back there and sending a different part of her here.

But when Ms Todd had done the trick on Ember, her body had been here. There was no body in the real world. She would just be missing, lost and gone, whereabouts unknown forever.

Would Harry think she'd run away, gone missing and never come home?

Oh.

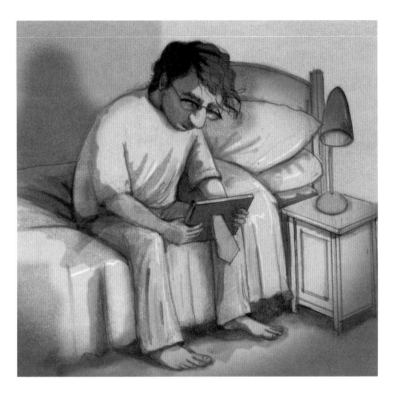

That thought, the thought of Harry not knowing where she was, of him forever wondering without finding an answer, was like turning to ice. She shivered with it. She felt the world plunge down the other side of the rollercoaster, her stomach levitating and empty and complaining.

Was it my fault? he'd think.

Oh.

'I'm glad you're here,' Ness said, breaking the spell of her thoughts. 'I was lonely. I was afraid. But now … now we're together again.'

She'd sat back down and was holding her hand out to Ember, gesturing at the spot on the step next to her. *Sit down,* she was saying, *sit down and stay.*

'No,' snapped Ember, who hadn't given up. 'No, we've got to go. Get up. Get up. There's still a way out, a way back.'

Ness shook her head.

'I don't think so. I'm too tired. Come and sit down. I'm cold.'

'Gah!'

It was frustration. She didn't like being angry with her friend; who did? But why was Ness being like this?

Yes, it had turned cold. Yes, she too felt tired, like a little nap wouldn't be so bad. But … they needed to get moving.

Ember pulled Ness up by the hand.

'Come on,' she said.

Ness didn't resist, but as soon as Ember stopped pulling, Ness stopped moving.

'I can't,' she murmured.

With her arm linked through Ness's arm, Ember marched her friend up the road.

It was slow-going.

Not just because they were arm in arm, and not just because they were tired, but because they seemed to be heading uphill.

There'd never been a hill here before, and if you looked you couldn't see one now, but that was how it felt.

And as they walked Ember noticed other ways in which the world seemed to have changed – changed with the change that had happened to her.

Someone had turned the lighting down: the whites of the black and white seemed dimmer, greyer, grimmer, and the blacks sharper, deeper, darker. It was as if night were falling, but the black sun still hadn't moved in the sky.

Either side of them a faint mist rolled that you could only see out of the corner of your eyes.

And the silence was no longer as silent.

Far off there was a sound like a continual rolling thunder or a moaning, or the shuffling of waves on a shore, or a train passing by in the deep of a summer's night. It was a mournful, dispiriting sound, whatever it was.

And inside Ember's chest her heart didn't beat.

There was no pulse at her wrist or neck.

Sometimes she forgot to breathe, and minutes went by and then she noticed and took a deep breath and it made no difference. Breathing was something the dead didn't need to do.

She felt like crying, but didn't. Dead tear ducts are dry.

The anger she had felt at first had long since evaporated.

All she felt now was a numbness, a blanketing boredom. And she knew, at last, how Ness had felt all along, all this time.

The girls said nothing as they walked past the school and the bakery and the newsagent's, nothing or nothing much.

Knowledge had arrived in Ember's mind when her life had vanished.

The dead know things.

She knew, for example, that there was no way out, no way back, no resurrection available.

That fact sat inside her like a twin sister, whispering to her.

Going through the gate, back to the colour of the alleys, would do to her what it had done to Betty. She would be not-dead and not-alive. The worst of both worlds.

Balance was the only thing that would work.

A swap. A deal. A trade.

A life for a life.

A death for a death.

One in. One out.

She didn't mention this to Ness. Didn't let on that this was all in vain. Was pointless, fruitless, hopeless. Had always been so.

She guessed Ness already knew.

The other thing Ember knew, though, was that if she stopped moving, if she stopped trying, then she would lose herself, lose all will to do anything.

And it would be so easy to stop.

So easy.

She felt bored and tired and cold.

She felt like she didn't care any more.

She told herself she cared.

Kept telling herself that.

But, really, she just wanted to close her eyes.

Being dead was so easy.

Just close your eyes.

Let go.

Go.

Eventually they turned into Uncle Graham's street.

It had been an effort.

The greyness was everywhere.

'Can't we just sit down?' Ness whispered. 'You and me, Deck. You and me. Just sit down over there. I'm so tired.'

She pointed at a shadowy patch of tarmac beside the sign that said the road's name, much like any other patch of tarmac.

'Of course we can't,' said Ember. 'We're so close. We'll be home soon.'

'I can't go home,' said Ness. 'I just want to sleep.'

Not in a million years would Ember admit that she felt the same urge.

It was like late at night, under the duvet, when the lights were out and the house was quiet and there was a CD playing with a story softly rolling out into the dark. She felt any moment now she'd be dreaming.

But at the same time she was cold, like the duvet was a winding sheet, damp and musty.

'Come on,' she said, pulling Ness up the road.

A cat-shaped smudge appeared in the air from nowhere, and in a second a dead mouse scuttled into its short afterlife, hopping away from the thing that had hitched a ride to the afterworld on the dying rodent's coat-tails.

The cat glowed, bright and multicoloured.

A searchlight had been switched on, a torch that shone in Ember's eyes.

Instinctively she lifted her arm to block the light.

'You?' she said.

'Me,' said the cat.

Ember snuck a look between her fingers.

The colours, the browns and dirty greys and patches of scuffed white and muddy orange, were dazzling, but slowly her eyes grew accustomed.

Although it was hard to look directly at the cat, she could glance at it and keep it at the edge of her vision without too much effort.

'You said you wouldn't come,' said Ember.

'A cat may change its mind,' said the cat.

The words 'A *cat may look at a queen*' came into her head and

she wondered why, where they were from … Was it a nursery rhyme?

'You've done it now,' the cat said. 'I warned you. She's not to be toyed with, that thing.'

'Ms Todd?'

The cat didn't answer the question, but said, 'What are you going to do now?'

'I don't know exactly,' she said. 'But I've still got that magic map thing. I'm gonna try to take us back.'

This was a lie, but she didn't know what else to say. The alternative was to sit down and forget everything.

'It won't work.'

Ember knew that.

'I've got to try.'

'Yes,' the cat said, rocking back and lifting one hind leg up high so it could nibble between the toes.

'Why do you say it won't work?'

She already knew, of course, but asking the question gave her something to push against. Something to feel.

'Rules,' said the cat, between mouthfuls. 'Always rules. In this world, in that world. Life has rules. Death has rules. The universe has rules.'

'Uncle Graham broke the rules,' she said. 'He came and got Betty.'

The cat said nothing, but moved on from its foot to its bum.

146

Ember knew what it meant, of course, even if she didn't want it to be true.

'Balance,' she said. 'That's a rule, isn't it?'

The cat made a noise that either meant 'Yes' or 'This bit's hard to get clean so I'm giving it an extra hard lick-nibble'.

She'd known it, of course.

They were both dead and they were both stuck.

The cat was right.

'How come you're here?' she asked again.

The cat lowered its leg, sat up straight, licking all round its mouth. It looked at her, its odd-coloured eyes blinking slowly.

'I like you,' it said with something like a shrug in its voice, as if it weren't a big deal, as if it didn't mean much.

It licked a front paw and rubbed it twice across an ear and an eye.

'Five minutes,' it said. 'Come to the house in five minutes. And be ready.'

With that it turned around, stepped behind itself and vanished.

Ember waited for Ness to say, 'What was that all about?' But she didn't say anything.

She'd let go of Ember's arm while the cat had been talking and had wandered away, not far, just over to the side of the road.

'Five minutes,' Ember said, looking at her watch.

The second hand didn't move. It read half past eight, the time she'd run down the alleys and into this place. She had no idea how long had passed since then, what time it would be back home now.

She hoped it wasn't too late.

She didn't want Harry to worry.

As they stood outside the house and looked at it, Ember felt something weird happen to her. It was as if her heart had beaten, just once, in her chest, and all the blood that had been sitting still in her veins had suddenly moved round. She shuddered.

She was being watched.

There *was* something in the house.

(She felt a shiver, a falling in her empty stomach. There was something wrong. A well that plunged into the dark below. Or meat left too long on the side.)

The front door was still propped open with the walking sticks and umbrellas. They looked funny lying there, such ordinary things.

'I can't go up there,' Ness whispered, pulling her arm away from Ember's. 'There's something there. I don't like it.'

'There's nothing there,' Ember lied. 'Come on, the cat's waiting.'

Be brave. Go on.

She took a step into the front garden, through the little gate, and stopped.

Was that a twitch of the net curtain? The front room's net curtain?

Had something tapped against the window?

Scraped the glass?

She couldn't say.

Had she seen a face in there?

She didn't think so, just the flicker of movement.

It was hard to know, the world being so dim and shadowy. (Had it grown dimmer and more shadowy as they'd walked here? Since they'd talked to the cat? Maybe. It was just so hard to tell.)

'Look, Ness, we've got to go in there.'

'No.'

'So what if there's someone in there? They're just a ghost, like us. Like what we are. I'm sure they won't do us any harm.'

Ember said the words calmly, even though she didn't believe them, or trust them. Even though she didn't know what they'd do when they got in there, when they got to the back gate. But someone had to take charge. Someone had to be brave. Someone had to be the one who pretended they knew what was going on, and today the job was hers.

Who could be in Uncle Graham's house?

Why would anyone choose to spend their afterlife there?

Whose house was this?

It had been her mum's childhood home, the house where Uncle Graham had looked after their parents when they got sick, long before December was born. And before then?

She was cold.

Oh.

As she took a step up the path, a dazzling, startling, shining light, like a motorbike headlight, hurtled out of the open front door, leapt high over the bundle of sticks and landed with the pad of soft feet on the ground.

It was the cat, running.

Ember felt the heat as it zoomed between her legs, and she turned, eyes stinging with the brightness of its aliveness, to see where it went, only to find it sat calmly on the ground beside Ness, looking up at her as if nothing was amiss.

'You're back,' she said.

'It took longer than expected,' the cat said. 'But you waited. Good.'

'What happens now?'

'You go through, December. You go home and it balances.'

There were noises inside the house, coming from behind the front door.

It was pulled open. Pulled wide.

Sticks clattered as the pile slumped.

Ember covered her eyes against the new light that burst from the doorway.

It was like a visitation, like a glowing alien emerging from its spacecraft, like an angel from an old myth come to share good news.

'You? You!' shouted a voice, disbelief spilling over the edges.

It was Uncle Graham.

How had he got here?

The cat had brought him.

That answer was easy enough to guess.

And then, from between his legs, a grey shape fell, snapping and chomping and dribbling.

Ember jumped aside and the dog lumbered past at speed, oblivious to her, focused on something else.

There was a hiss and a flash of claws and the dog barked and whimpered at the same time as the cat leapt up on to the garden wall and simply ignored the slobbering thing. It looked the other way. Licked at its front paw.

Betty scratched at the wall frantically, bouncing on her hind legs, but she wasn't tall enough.

'Down, girl,' snapped Uncle Graham.

The dog stopped jumping, but growled and whined, paced back and forth, turning in pathetic circles, all the while glaring up at the cat and dribbling ghastly black and white dribble.

Then Uncle Graham looked at Ember properly.

'What's happened?' he said. 'You're all … grey.'

He waved his hand at her, as if showing her herself.

'Ms Todd,' said Ember.

'Her?' he said, in a voice that spat.

'Yes,' she replied.

'She's a lying piece of work,' he said. 'Don't trust her.'

He shook his head.

'No,' Ember said.

As they spoke she had been thinking.

The cat had brought Uncle Graham here for a purpose, for a reason.

Now, here, in the world of the dead, there was a *living person*.

That meant that one of the dead could leave, could go back down the alleys, so long as Uncle Graham remained behind.

Balance.

That was what the cat had said.

But, she thought, the cat wanted *her* to go home. It had brought her uncle here in order to let *her* live again.

Like Ms Todd, the cat wasn't thinking about Ness.

But …

She didn't want to go home *alone*. The *whole point* of this had been to find Happiness, to take *her* back, to *bring* her back. What would the point be if she went back without her very best friend?

And the answer spun in her: no point at all.

'Ness,' she said, turning to the faded girl by the wall, and speaking softly but quickly. 'You need to go through the house. I'll distract my uncle. You run! Go out the back and down the alley. It'll take you home … Quickly, go now.'

Ness didn't move.

'I'm scared,' she whispered, almost too quiet for Ember to hear.

The cat had jumped down and led Betty a merry dance across the road, to the gardens on the other side, and Uncle Graham had followed, trying to keep his dog under control. Trying to keep her safe from this strange and dangerous cat, as he saw it.

But now he had turned, come back towards the girls, huddled in their conspiracy. The colour and light spilt from him, hurting their eyes and making Ness cower.

'What's going on?' he shouted.

Ember thought that he must know what she was thinking. How could he *not* see what her plan was? It was so obvious. Obvious, but the only plan she could think of.

But it seemed he didn't.

'Amber,' he said, 'what's going on? What's all this muttering about?'

He was standing on the pavement, and Betty had slumped herself by his feet.

The girls were in the front garden, the front door behind them.

If they could get in the house, Ember could keep her uncle away while Ness ran for the back door. She could give her friend enough time to get away before her uncle, bigger and stronger than her, got into the house.

Her unbeating heart was light now she'd made her decision.

Ness had a dad and a mum and a big brother, she had cousins who came to visit, lots of grandparents, she was much better at being friends with the kids at school, she was going to be a doctor or a vet or an actor one day ... she had so much to live for, so many people who were missing her back home ... and all Ember had was Harry ... not that this was maths, it wasn't just a sum, balancing this side with that, but Ember wanted more than anything for her friend to be alive again, to no longer be just this shadow of the girl, this echo, this bored grey whisper ... and even if that meant she, Ember, wouldn't get to see it, it didn't mean it wasn't still the right thing to do ...

What did they call it? When you gave something up to help someone else?

There were clouds around her. Grey. Heavy. Dull.

Forget the word, she thought, *just run*.

'Quick,' she said, pushing Ness ahead of her. 'Run!'

Through the door.

Into the hall.

Tripping, slipping on the clatter of sticks and umbrellas.

The two girls, the two ghost girls, fell and rolled across the floor.

A rattle like hail falling.

December spun in place and began pulling the sticks away.

She had to close the door. Get it shut quick.

She could see her uncle moving from the pavement to the front garden.

Heading for her, for the door. For her.

Through the gap, as she scrabbled frantically, she saw a thought cross his shining face.

That face like a flaming beacon, that face filled with life in this grey place, had a thought on it, a memory, a realisation suddenly settling, suddenly understanding itself at last.

He knew, she knew, that if the front door shut he would be locked out.

And he would be shut here, trapped here, to wither forever among the dead.

He began to run as Ember pulled the last umbrella away and threw herself, from her knees, at the door, slamming it shut.

Crash!

He thudded into it. Outside.

They were safe.

He banged at the door, hammered at it, called her name, but she was safe. For the moment.

She turned to Ness, who hadn't helped her, and saw that the moment of safety had been a short one indeed.

Somehow, perhaps in that last split second when she'd thrown herself at the door, Betty had got in. Running ahead of her master, grey and unnoticed, she had slipped through the closing gap, and now she was growling at Ness, who was lying where she had fallen on the hall floor.

Circling round, staring and snarling, the dog dripped grey drops of dribble on to the carpet.

She was between the girls and the kitchen, her wide shoulders blocking the corridor, her grey eyes glinting with violence.

Ness had enough sense left in her to back away, shuffling up the hall, inching away from those jaws that snapped but didn't bite.

Ember climbed to her feet and pushed herself to think.

Had she been alive, adrenalin would have been pumping through her veins, surging her thoughts quicker, her breaths faster, her fear higher, but grey as she was it took effort to even remember the urgency. The need for haste slipped away if she didn't keep reminding herself.

She pinched her arm, like a dreamer.

There was a battering on the front door, and then it stopped.

A moment's silence, and then Betty barked.

She was getting bolder. She wanted her master back, maybe. Was afraid of the girls, maybe. Felt cornered, perhaps.

Ember looked around for a way out.

They could run through, run past the dog, for the kitchen, but that seemed too dangerous.

Up the stairs, but that seemed too far, and too dark.

And so, without real thought, simply for a moment's safety, she grabbed Ness by the arm, dragged her up on to her feet and dodged through the half-open door at their side, into the front room.

Click!

The door shut behind her as she leant on it.

Betty banged it from the other side, barked twice, and then there was silence.

Or not quite silence.

There was the crackle, the hiss in the air that December had noticed in the house before. It came from in here, from this room, and she finally understood what it was.

In the bay window was a television, a big, old-fashioned one that took up a whole table.

Its screen showed static. Black and white dancing.

Facing the television, away from the girls, was a wing-backed armchair, tall, tatty and grey.

All she could see of the occupant was a woman's hand resting on the arm. Pale. Clad in thin, patterned cloth. A bracelet with small stones set in flower-shaped mounts.

For a moment the flowers looked blue, but that had just been a trick of the mind. They were as grey as everything else.

The hand didn't move.

Ness was shaking.

Ember's heart lurched again, a single great pump sloshing blood through her veins.

She felt sick.

Betty barked twice, out in the hallway.

Not knowing why, not understanding her feet, Ember stepped closer … towards the television, towards the chair.

The room was laid out differently from the same room back in Uncle Graham's house. Everything seemed older, from another decade, another century. There was no dog basket.

Ember saw the grey face of the woman in the chair.

Be brave. Go on.

She was watching the static on the TV, gaunt and distant and lost.

She didn't notice Ember.

She was a young woman, but so very dead. A young face, with long dark hair, like someone falling away underwater, drowning and sinking and staring.

'What is it?' said Ness.

A whisper.

Nervous.

Shaking.

'It's my mum,' said Ember.

She stood there for a long time, wondering what to do.

　Ness lingered in the background.

　Just the hiss of static.

21

And then –

A crash at the window. Glass not quite smashing, but cracking, rattling in the frame.

Ember knew she should have jumped. Any red-blooded girl would have jumped at the sudden sound. But her blood was grey, and because she'd been staring so hard at the woman in the chair she hadn't any spare attention to be surprised.

Nevertheless, she looked round.

There at the window Uncle Graham's hands and face were looking in, from beyond the net curtain.

It was like the sun had risen.

Light poured in.

'Gray?'

This, a voice of cobwebs and smoke.

The woman in the chair looked up and a wavering hand

pointed at the window.

'Gray?' she said again.

Uncle Graham vanished, went off looking for some other way in.

Greyness washed the room once more.

In Ember's chest her heart gave another sluggish thud.

'Mum?' she said quietly.

It took a few seconds, years, for the word to cross the gap between them, but once it had the woman in the chair slowly turned her head.

The eyes! Ember thought. *Those are my eyes.*

Another moment passed by with just the hiss of the television for company.

The woman's hair drifted round her head, and her mouth moved soundlessly, searching for the right words.

And then she spoke.

'Em?' she said. 'Is that you?'

'Yes,' said Ember.

'Oh,' said her mother.

A hand lifted up from the arm of the chair, hovered in the space between them.

'You've grown,' she said. 'You've grown so beautiful.'

The words were slow, tiptoed into the air.

Ember didn't know what to say. She didn't move. She didn't breathe.

Her mother looked liked the photos of her, but greyer, lost at the edges.

She was the age she'd been in the photo of the three of them, when Ember was really small.

Yet another surge of blood lurched through her veins, making her feel, making her burn.

She glanced at Ness, but her friend was cowering by the door. She was looking away, looking as if she were about to turn the handle. She didn't want to be there.

Ness had never met Ember's mum. The girls had met years after she'd died.

Maybe Ness wanted to give them some time together, some space. Maybe she was just being polite.

'Mum,' said Ember, 'this is my best friend, Happiness Browne.'

Her mum turned slowly, leant out and peered round the corner of the armchair.

'Both dead,' she sighed, looking from one girl to the other.

'Oh.

Both lost.'

A pause.

'Em, how did it happen? You're so young still. How did you come here so soon? How ... ?'

Ember looked down at herself.

She was dead. She'd nearly forgotten, for the moment.

It was almost enough to make you laugh.

'No,' she said, shaking her head. 'I didn't die. No. You see, I'm not *really* dead. It's a mistake, a misunderstanding.'

But she *was* dead.

She explained, as much as she could, what had happened. Ness. Betty. Uncle Graham. Ms Todd.

'And now that cat's helped us,' Ember said. 'The cat's brought everyone here. And I've got to get Ness out the back door before Uncle Graham finds a way in. She's got to go back.'

Her mum stood, tall and desperate, and stepped over to Ness and said, 'Thank you, little one.'

Ness shrank under the words, kind as they seemed to Ember.

And her mum reached down and turned the door handle, which crumbled as she touched it.

The door swung open, just as the front room window exploded in a shower of flying glass, and something huge and solid and real fell to the carpet, shining and shouting with light.

Uncle Graham had got in.

'Ness! Run!' Ember shouted.

Her uncle grabbed her arm.

The burning was intense, there where his fingers touched.

He didn't hold her hard, but just the warmth of his blood, the heat of the life in him, tormented her.

Thoughts swirled in her, caught in a flood, confused, confusing thoughts that muddled and bumped together, jostling, making no sense: maybe she could distract her uncle long enough for Ness to get home; or maybe she could distract him long enough for her mum to get home (wouldn't Harry be happy to see her again?); or she could fight free and run home herself, pushing everyone else aside; or she could stay and spend the rest of her dead-life wandering the ghost world, exploring; or she could be with her mum; or her mum could save her, somehow; or Harry could save her; or she could wake up and find that this was all a dream;

or … oh, Ness!

Her eyes were blurry, not filled with tears, because tears wouldn't come, but with panic and pain.

She sank to her knees.

His burning fingers held her.

'Get away from the door, you,' he was saying. 'Out of the way.'

He was talking to Ness, she thought.

And then there was a whoosh, like a cold wind, that cut through Ember, right to her bones, and he let go of her. His fingers let her slip.

A wind whispered, 'She's mine!'

Ember fell to the floor, crumpled, clutching her arm in her cool, numb hand.

Uncle Graham yelled.

He was flapping wildly, like Hollie Adams did in the playground when a bee got too close to her.

Ember looked up and he was wrapped in a ghost, tangled in the seaweed tendrils of her mum's dress, of her arms, her sleeves, her hair. Wreathing and roiling and wrapping. A shipwrecked figurehead refusing to let go.

The light had slowed down.

They were struggling and he was losing, his efforts growing weaker with each moment, with each movement.

Ember couldn't see her mother's face – she had her back to her – but she was afraid of it, all the same.

Gunpowder.

Oh, she understood Ness's fear of the long-dead woman. She was awful, wilful, unforgiving. A pit going down and down, bottomless. Oh! Poor Uncle Graham!

And she shivered with the knowledge of what it was like to touch the living. How Uncle Graham's life, how his blood and breath and heat, burned, scorched … how it hurt. Oh! Her poor mother!

Ice, becoming slush.

And then her mum stepped back, drifted back, let go. Opened her arms and stepped back, and her uncle staggered against the wall, dazed, lost, ashen and gasping for breath.

Pale as a ghost.

He was confusion, forgetfulness, fear.

He pushed himself away from the wall, not looking at anyone, not seeing anyone, not hearing anything but the thud of his heart. And as he pushed he touched Ness, pushed her against the wall under his hand, and she slid away as he fell through the open doorway into the hall …

And then he was gone, vanished off down the passage, to the kitchen, to the garden, to the …

And her mum shrank down, just a woman again, drifting gently with the current; her hair flowing, her eyes looking away.

And Ness continued sliding along the wall, her eyes clear and wide and staring.

'Deck,' she said in a calm, faraway whisper, 'there's something wrong. Something wrong here ... I don't feel ... I don't feel anything ...'

And then she fell to the floor, but like someone sitting down after climbing a long flight of stairs, not like someone collapsing, and she looked up at Ember one final time, her eyes almost brown, and flashing, and then she looked away, distracted, and crumpled, faded, sifted into a girl-shaped heap of dust.

And then the heap itself faded, shrank, blew away, grain by grain, on a wind that Ember didn't feel, on a wind that moved nothing else in the room, that blew from nowhere to nowhere.

'No,' she said, gasping.

'No!'

And then her mother was beside her, in front of her, staring into her eyes.

'Em, dear,' she said in a whisper, 'it's just us now.'

Ember was struggling.

'But ...

    Ness ...

        she ...'

The words didn't work.

Dust on the wind, said her mother's eyes, which were her eyes.

A pause …

then …

her mum reached down, blouse rippling like kelp, and embraced her.

Held her tight.

Held her there.

Held her forever.

And December's tearless eyes wept for Happiness.

Days passed like a dream, held in those arms, lowered, hunched, crouched together on the living-room floor.

At one point Betty waddled into the room.

She looked around, greyness looking at greyness, and sadly waddled over to the pair of them.

Her master had gone.

She'd been left alone again, and being still a dog at heart, alone was the one thing she couldn't bear. Anything but that. Anything but *alone*.

Without asking, without seeming to think anything was strange, Betty waddled forward and slumped with a *crumph* beside them, leaning hard and heavy and cold against Ember's side, and then she laid that big head of hers on the girl's lap.

Her mum gently, idly, stroked the dog's face.

'Such a pretty one,' she whispered. 'Good old Gray.'

And so, then they were three.

And then, after a while, they were two again, as the dog's dust was lifted up on an unfelt wind.

And Ember thought, *She wasn't such a bad dog,* as she wiped ghostly dribble off her trousers. *She was mostly made of love.*

And endless time passed by.

What was left?

Ness was gone and Betty was gone and Uncle Graham had left them all.

He'd run off, out the house, through the garden and back to the real world.

She could feel it.

She'd come here to save Ness, but with Ness gone she could have saved herself. And that had been the cat's plan all along, after all: leave Uncle Graham here and let dead December flee back to the light. But the chance had passed by. The chance had gone.

Her mum was humming, a tune she had never heard before.

'He could have saved you,' Ember whispered eventually.

'What?' said her mum.

'Uncle Graham,' she said. 'He brought me here to get his dog back. To rescue Betty. He made a deal with someone … with that Ms Todd, I think … that let him swap a living person for a dead one.'

Her mum said nothing.

'He could have done it back then, though, couldn't he? He could have saved you. I would've. You know I would've if I could've. I'd've been here in a flash, or Harry would've …'

'Em, darling,' her mum said. 'You were tiny. There was nothing you could do. Nor Harry. And don't blame Gray either. Without him, I'd not ever have seen you again. We wouldn't be together now, would we?'

Rustling leaves. A breeze in autumn. Falling leaves.

'I waited,' her mum said. 'For so long. I held on. Dreaming, perhaps. Days or years or minutes or hours. Time is strange. Look how big you got … How did that happen?' She leant back and brushed a strand of hair away from Ember's eyes, stroked her cheek. 'When did you get so big? Oh.'

Ember felt like she was falling asleep, was warm in bed, although it was cold.

The black and white world around her was dimming, growing fainter. Just a room now. Just them.

She smiled.

'We are together,' her mum said.

'Yes,' whispered Ember.

For years she had wondered if she'd have anything to say to her mum were she ever to meet her. She'd imagined her like a movie star, like someone you know off the telly, who you recognise, who seems so familiar, but who you don't really know at all. Who doesn't know you. She'd expected to be tongue-tied and embarrassed. But it wasn't like that. Not like that at all.

There were things she wanted to tell her mum, about her and Harry, and about school and about holidays, and about Ness, and about moving house, and about Tilda and Porkpie, and about what was happening in her favourite shows on TV, and about what had happened in the soaps her mum had liked in all the years since she'd stopped watching them.

There was so much to say, and she didn't need to say any of it.

Not a word.

She just wanted to sit quiet and safe in that embrace.

They could be quiet together, and that was a gift.

'We've all the time in the world,' her mum said, reading her mind.

It made sense.

Ember felt so sleepy.

Her eyes were closing.

Neither hot nor cold now.

Just dim. Fuzzy.

She'd had her life, hadn't she? She'd been happy. She'd been loved. She'd lived enough, hadn't she? It hadn't been bad.

'Stay with me,' her mum whispered. 'You belong with me. You were always mine.'

Her voice was barely a breath.

'Stay here.'

She began humming that tune again.

Ember slept, or sort of slept, deep in her mother's arms for the first time in what might have been centuries.

And that long night went on.

Eventually, suddenly, the sun rose in December's dream, a startling dawn, too early, filled with birdsong and summer haze. It washed away sleep, comfort, forgetting.

'Get away from her,' said a voice from out of the light.

Ember knew that voice.

She stumbled closer to wakefulness.

Despite the light, despite the summeriness, she felt cold, weighed down.

'Leave her be,' said the voice. 'She is not yours.'

She knew the voice.

She was treading water, struggling to get her head into the air.

There was a hiss and flash of claws and fire and December was thrown up on to the riverbank, and she found she was in the front room, lying on the rug that covered the floorboards, staring at its grey pattern.

The cat was stood between her and her mother, its light spilling out, filling their faces.

She covered her eyes, blinked hard and saw her mother high above her.

'No. Em,' she said, 'we are together again. At last, it's us.'

'Run, girl,' the cat said calmly, firmly, simply. 'Go home. People are waiting for you. Your supper's waiting and it's still hot. Run, now.'

Ember backed away. She saw her mother for what she was, for what she had become: a ghost, long-lost herself, deep underwater.

The cat hissed.

'Too long,' it said, looking at the dead woman.

'Far too long.'

Ember climbed to her feet. Sense climbed into her head.

She wasn't meant to be dead.

This was her last chance to run.
She took a step towards the door,
but there was a knot she couldn't
untie.

'I can't,' she said, surprising herself.
'You don't understand, cat.
That's my mum.'

'And she's dead, girl,' the cat said, not turning away from the woman. 'And you don't have to be. Look to the living. Look to the living now. It's not your time to be here.'

She was torn in pieces.

'Run.'

She didn't.

'I heard what you were thinking, girl. The word you wanted was "sacrifice", and you would've done it. I can see you. I can see into you. I know you better than you know. You would've done it for her, now I will do it for you.'

'What?'

'I will stay,' the cat said. 'I am alive. You are dead. That is the deal. I will stay; you will go.'

Ember's heart gave a sudden single, surging beat.

'Do not even think to argue.'

Blood heaved in her.

Hope heaved.

'Do not linger.'

She didn't want to stay here.

She didn't want to be dead any more.

'Em,' her mother said, leaning down beside her. 'Stay.'

She laid a hand on Ember's shoulder.

For such a grey and washed-out dead woman, the grip was astonishingly strong, astonishingly tight, astonishingly cold.

Dust and electricity and ice.

Love, turned to an anchor, turned to seaweed, turned to bindweed.

Ember couldn't move.

She tugged, but it was no good.

'Oh,' she said, feeling suddenly, finally, endlessly, defeated.

She looked at the cat.

'It has to be you,' the cat said. 'I cannot do this.'

Ember tried to wriggle free, tried to shake her mother off, but the arms came around her, embraced her, surrounded her.

'Em,' said a whisper in her ear. 'Don't leave me. Don't leave me again.'

Each word was a knife.

'No,' said Ember.

Instinctively she gulped worthless air into empty lungs, like someone about to be dragged under.

'I've been waiting,' her mother whispered. 'You made me wait so long. So long.'

'No,' Ember whispered.

'You can't … you can't leave me. Don't leave me. Not again.'

The arms wrapped round her like smoke, fogging her and choking her. Drowning her. Pulling her. Down, down, down.

She struggled and pushed back helplessly.

Her heart gave another thump; another jolt of blood surged in her veins, burning her insides with life.

And then …

'No!' she shouted. 'No!' She twisted and turned in the icy embrace. 'It wasn't me,' she gasped. 'It wasn't *me* who left *you*. It wasn't *me*. I didn't go away. Mum! It wasn't *me* who left.'

And with that final shout, that expulsion of truth, of heart, of honesty, tears came to her dry eyes and a breeze came up from nowhere and a tickling crossed her arms and face and she collapsed forwards, no longer held up, no longer pinned down. A shadow lifted, a memory flew away, a forgetfulness fell.

And then …

dust

… it was just her and the cat in the front room.

She sat there for a long time as the cat paced and sat and paced and washed.

In time she stood up. Exhausted. Emptied out.

The cat watched as she went to the kitchen.

'Harry's probably waiting,' she said to the room.

The cat nodded. Walked behind her.

In the garden it trotted in front of her, dug in a flowerbed, turned and looked at her.

'I don't expect to see you for a long time,' it said.

'What will you do?' she said.

'This and that,' said the cat. 'Sleep, maybe.'

'But this place,' she said.

The cat looked around.

'All places are alike to me,' it said. 'Here or there, it doesn't much matter. The quiet will be nice.'

She had reached the gate and turned the handle.

The alley was filled with colour.

'Ms Todd?' she said.

The cat said nothing, but it filled in the hole it had made and jumped up on to the fence.

The last Ember saw of it was a flash of colour vanishing into next door's garden like a sunset.

Oh, she thought. I *didn't say thank you.*

She let the gate click shut behind her.

She hurried to the first corner and walked round it, past the bins to the next corner.

She was without Happiness, but somehow that was all right.

It was all wrong, of course, but also it was all right.

As she turned the third corner, her heart started beating again, and didn't stop.

Ember ran through the night.

It was almost eleven o'clock (her watch had caught up with the real world as soon as she'd returned).

She got home just after Harry and Penny.

She hid behind a parked car and watched them unlock the door and let themselves in.

As soon as the door was shut she scampered across, lifted the letterbox flap and peered through.

Harry had gone into the front room and Penny was heading off down the hall through the kitchen to the bathroom at the back.

As soon as she was out of sight, Ember slipped the spare key into the door and, with tiptoeing movements, opened it slowly.

She slipped in and left the door slightly ajar. (To shut it you always had to bang it because the lock was stiff.)

She could hear Harry and her grandparents talking, about the play and about the evening and she heard the words, 'No trouble at all. Not heard a peep all night. Good as gold.'

And at that Ember ran up the stairs two at a time, avoiding the squeaky third step, and was under the covers (with her shoes on) by the time her dad opened her door.

She pretended to sleep.

It was only once he'd kissed her on the head and gone out again that she began to fiddle with her shoelaces.

They had knots and in the end she just slipped them off, still tied, and let them fall to the floor for Harry to deal with in the morning.

Then she lay in the dark and cried, real tears. Wet tears. Salt tears.

Happiness was gone, and she hadn't even said goodbye to her. She was *really* gone and nothing was going to bring her back. Not this time, no matter how clever Ember was, no matter how much she wished it.

There was a hole in her middle, and she fell down it.

She thought of her mum too, as she fell.

She thought of the picture of her on the mantelpiece that she'd always loved, not what she had become. It was surprisingly easy to let go of the memory of what had happened in that afterworld. The knowledge that her mum had waited was enough to know. The rest she could forget. Let go of.

Yes. Letting go. Let it go.

And so she cried.

Big sobs, like the dead deserve.

But, in time, she was all cried out, and she turned her pillow over to the dry side and tried to sleep.

December didn't go to school on Monday, because it was the day of the funeral. The weather was suitably grey and blustery and she wore her smartest, darkest clothes.

There were a few other kids from school there, but she didn't speak to them. She just sat with Harry and Penny and was quiet. It was what she wanted to do.

At the front Mr and Mrs Browne sat quietly too. Ness's big brother had come back from university to be with them. He sat there, in a suit that didn't quite fit, with his head in his hands.

The coffin was brought in and they all stood up and then they all sat down again.

Someone said some words she didn't really hear, and then a cousin of Ness's that Ember had never seen before stood up and sang a song that she'd written for the guitar. And then they all stood up and sang a song, and then they all sat down again. Ness's grandad, who Ember had never met either, stood and said a lot of words about her, about how good she was and how kind and all that sort of thing.

She remembered some of the things Ness had told her, some of the stories she'd told her about him, and she smiled, almost laughed, in fact.

Then they played some music, and the coffin trundled off through some curtains into a hole in the wall and she knew that that was where it would be burned.

Everyone cried, and then afterwards they went to a nearby pub, where the Brownes had laid on some food.

Even though Ember wasn't hungry she ate three sausage rolls, four little triangular sandwiches, a stale salted peanut and several handfuls of crisps out of politeness.

Before they left she went up to Ness's mum, Mrs Browne, and said, 'I'm sorry.'

She didn't know what else to say.

I *tried?*

Mrs Browne didn't need to know that.

She just said, 'Thank you, Amber, dear,' and dabbed her eyes with a soggy handkerchief.

No one corrected her. It wasn't the time.

'Come on,' said Harry quietly, his hand on her shoulder.

They headed for the exit, but halfway there Ember turned and ran back to Ness's mum.

'Mrs Browne?' she asked.

'Yes?'

'Can I ask … ? I've a question …'

'Yes?'

'When they give you the dust, can I –'

'Dust?'

'You know, from the coffin and …'

'The ashes?'

Mrs Browne choked as she said the words.

'Can I … Can you give me a bit? Just a little. She was my *best* friend, and I want to, you know, scatter a bit of her in the garden.'

It was what people did, wasn't it? Harry had scattered her mum's ashes in the woods where they sometimes walked, where the bluebells came out in the spring.

Mrs Browne was silent, as if she didn't know what to say.

'Of course you can,' said Mr Browne, putting a hand on his wife's shoulder. His eyes were huge and shining, still and deep and reflective as hammer ponds. 'Can't she, Hazel? Ember was all that Ness would talk about. She loved you, you know.'

'Of course,' repeated Mrs Browne.

'It'll be a few days,' Mr Browne said. 'I'll bring them round.'

'Thank you,' said Ember, not feeling in the least bad about the lie she'd told them.

She had no intention of scattering Ness's dust. She'd seen her ashes scattered already. She wanted to keep some of it together, keep it safe. That was all. She had no plan to do anything with it. She just wanted to have her friend close.

With a tear rolling down her cheek and a red nose, she walked back to Harry and Penny and took them each by the hand and walked with them out into the car park, out into the cool spring afternoon, out into the rest of their days together. Happy days.

Not to be forgotten.

Not to be rushed through.

Not to be wasted.

Praise for *The Imaginary*

'By turns scary and funny, touching without being sentimental, and beautifully illustrated by Emily Gravett, *The Imaginary* is a delight from start to finish'

Financial Times

'A moving read about loyalty and belief in the extraordinary'

Guardian

'The kind of children's book that's the reason why adults should never stop reading children's books. Touching, exciting and wonderful to look at (Emily Gravett's illustrations are incredible), I absolutely adored this. And I cried a little bit'

Robin Stevens

'A glorious delight … Loved it!'

Jeremy Strong

'Packed full of heart'

Phil Earle, *Guardian*

'This is young fiction of the very best quality, showcasing inspiration, inventiveness and an intoxicating passion for storytelling. *The Imaginary* has the potential to be a family favourite and a future classic'

BookTrust

'A richly visualised story which explores imaginary friends and the very special role they play in children's lives. Emily Gravett's illustrations capture the hazy world of the imaginaries brilliantly'

Julia Eccleshare, Lovereading4kids

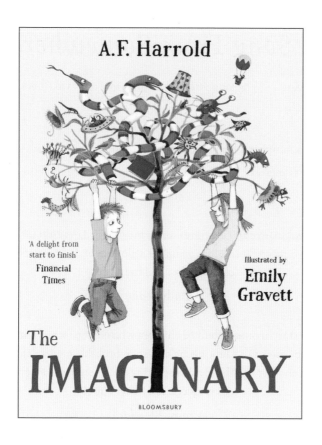

RUDGER IS AMANDA'S BEST FRIEND.

HE DOESN'T EXIST.

BUT NOBODY'S PERFECT.

Winner of the UKLA 2016 Book Award in the 7–11 category

Longlisted for the CILIP Carnegie Medal
and the Kate Greenaway Medal 2016

Praise for
The Song From Somewhere Else

'Extraordinary ... as moving, strange and profound as David Almond's *Skellig*'

Guardian

'Broodingly atmospheric black-and-white illustrations by Levi Pinfold ... the tale turns into a fantasy of another world, blending the strange and the everyday'

Sunday Times

'Wildly imaginative and heartbreakingly moving ... Levi Pinfold's superbly evocative, misty illustrations complete a glorious and unforgettable tale of loyalty, loss and friendship'

Daily Mail

'A curious story about two bullied children who end up forming an unlikely friendship based on a haunting melody, an improbable mother, an invasion from another world and a disappearing cat. There are wonderfully evocative pictures by Levi Pinfold'

Evening Standard

'What begins as a story of bullying becomes a whirlpool of mystery as Frank tries to undo the damage she has done. A magic story of friendship and love, with atmospheric black-and-white illustrations by Levi Pinfold'

Irish Examiner

'There is a delicate sensibility, a happy strangeness, to this; sometimes scary, sometimes funny, always essential. The illustrations by Pinfold – black and white, pencil, dramatic and evocative – are a vital component'

Big Issue

SOMETIMES YOU FIND FRIENDSHIP WHERE YOU LEAST EXPECT IT.

Longlisted for the CILIP Carnegie Medal
and shortlisted for the Kate Greenaway Medal 2018

Winner of the Amnesty CILIP Honour 2018